The Misadventures of Arnold the Armadillo

By Paul Jannereth

Illustrated by Ellen Jannereth
Creative Editing by Andy Jannereth
Editing by Venessa Baez & Alyssa Layton

by the sea ™

Publications

For contact information and updates, please visit
www.Facebook.com/ilovearnoldthearmadillo

After writing each chapter of this book, I got to spend quality time with my kids as we discussed the story and how it could be improved. It has been a thrill to hear them laugh out loud and offer such wonderful and creative suggestions. What a precious gift it has been. This book was written for them, and I am so proud of their love of books, love of life, and now for a character they helped to create – Arnold the Armadillo.

This book is dedicated to Ellen and Andy.

All my love

Arnold's Armadillo Tales

Chapter 1

Under The Garden Wall

"There. I would go 'there' as opposed to 'here', but that's just me. I was walking 'there' and once I got 'there' it was now 'here'. But I still preferred 'there', which continued to be elusive, and so I kept moving. Here, there, everywhere! But it must be something, and something must be somewhere, but where? There? Yes, 'there' is where. I will go 'there' as opposed to 'here', but that's just me..."

Such were the thoughts racing through Arnold's mind as he frantically sniffed the ground in search of a mid-afternoon snack. Something smelled really good to him and his three older friends, Willie, Mitch, and Irene, as they bumped and prodded their way forward and around, sometimes bumping into each other as they moved frantically toward the back of the yard. They looked almost as if they were dancing, excitement raced through their bodies as if it was Christmas morning! But it was a damp and cool spring afternoon, a time when the rain refreshed the air with a crispness that excited the senses and energized the body of an armadillo into a frenzy. This excitement had brought them far from their home and into a new territory. They were not aware of how far they had traveled, since armadillo's cannot see much past a few feet. But that smell could have been a mile away and they'd have sensed it. It was something similar to a turkey dinner on Thanksgiving, and from wherever it was coming they were being instinctively and irresistibly drawn. Their noses were telling an irresistible tale of happiness, joy, and adventure!

Arnold and his friends could sense that they were very near to whatever tasty goodies had been calling to them like their own personal Lorelei. And like that mystical sea maiden that would tempt sailors with her irresistible beauty, Arnold was unknowingly being drawn into a long and dangerous journey of his own. They were growing tired but they never stopped moving, so strong was the wonderful scent, the alluring call. Then, without warning, SMACK! Arnold had slammed his head right up against a garden wall. Willie then slammed into his behind, and Irene into his, followed then by Mitch who always seemed to be last. It was a painful chain of armadillos crashing into each other, then scattering around stunned as if they had just woke from a dream and back into reality.

"I didn't see that coming!" Arnold shouted in stunned amazement.

"Of course you didn't, none of us did," retorted an angry Willie. "We armadillos can't see much better than a bat!"

"But I can smell it! So fresh, so close!" Irene proclaimed. "It has to be right here!"

As each of them struggled to understand what had happened, their confusion began to leave them frustrated. Finally, Arnold began to dig frantically into the ground at the base of the garden wall.

"What are you digging for? China?" cried Willie as the rest broke out in laughter. "This isn't the place to dig; the smell is coming from over top the wall. We need to find a way around this thing." So the others began to sniff around, Willie and Irene going toward the right and Mitch toward the left, leaving Arnold alone and digging frantically downward. Even Arnold didn't really understand why he was suddenly digging straight down; the smell was certainly not coming from below. But he became obsessed, and the digging became more frantic as dirt began to shoot out from this little creature's legs straight up and behind him like a geyser! It was a queer site to behold, and unbeknownst to the armadillos, someone from above was watching.

Mrs. Widmer noticed the dirt flailing up into the air as she sat at her kitchen table enjoying an afternoon cup of warm tea on the damp rainy day. She couldn't see the ground which was hidden by several small bushes, but the flying dirt produced a surge of rage which pulsed through her body like a bolt of lightning! Her tea cup landed hard upon the saucer, the spoon jumping from it off onto the table. She leapt up from the table and dashed over to the back door to investigate.

Mrs. Widmer was an older woman, a widow, who had devoted her retirement years to creating the most exquisite garden in the neighborhood. There were flowers, annuals, shrubs, trees, pathways, garden gnomes, ornaments, bird baths, and a couple of small fountains... Mrs. Widmer was happiest when her world was quiet, peaceful, and neatly arranged just that way she wanted. She lived alone with her little Yorkie dog, Penni, who would stroll around her master's garden, decorated with delicate pink little ribbons in her hair. Penni was a terribly sensitive doggie with even the slightest disturbance able to send her crying back toward the house. But at first, Penni misinterpreted Mrs. Widmer's sudden dash toward the back door as a rare playful adventure! But then Penni paused and began to shiver as Mrs. Widmer gazed out the back door window, beginning to tie the belt of her robe around her waist, preparing to go outside.

Meanwhile, Arnold was making incredible progress as the other armadillos had quickly given up on finding a way around the wall, and had circled back and were now just simply watching Arnold launching piles of dirt and mud high into the air. Small stones, old acorns, and the occasional worm treat flew out from the deep hole inside which Arnold now was completely immersed. One worm landed directly on Irene's nose! She quickly snapped it up and chewed the thick little worm up for a tasty snack.

"Thank you Arnold!" she shouted. The others now were content to sit there and wait for Arnold to throw up other morsels of earthly goodness. By now dirt was covering the entire area and Arnold was almost completely out of sight. Just then, the door to Mrs. Widmer's house suddenly slammed shut! She was on her way, but the armadillo is slow to react to outside noises, especially when a treasure of rain drenched food was so close at hand. Mrs. Widmer approached the bushes armed with a broom and expecting to find the two little children from next door doing some awful damage to her lovely garden. She had caught them before, climbing over her wall and walking through her yard's beautiful array of flowers and bushes. The little girl was always looking for beautiful new flowers to collect, and the little boy for exciting bugs and geckos to capture. Mrs. Widmer stealthily approached the garden wall where

Penni

Arnold was still digging. She slowly passed the first of three bird houses and a large concrete bird bath complete with a little running fountain. There were several well placed little garden gnomes along the well edged landscaping, making it the perfect setting to pass a most tranquil afternoon tea. Mrs. Widmer was very protective of her precious garden and all its various delicate decorations. And she was in no mood to politely deal with little children who were creating such a mess!

Arnold was still digging when the broom came sweeping down upon his friends who quickly scattered in all directions. Mrs. Widmer shouted in fright as she suddenly realized that these were not children at all, but armadillos! Penni, watching safely from the back door window, also gave a sharp squeal of fright! Mrs. Widmer gave chase and pursued them across her beautiful garden, taking large swipes with her broom at every opportunity in order to drive out the armadillo pack! She swung with large open sweeps striking flowers and blooms and launching flower peddles high into the air and scattering in all directions! She tore along the garden wall following Willie and Mitch who suddenly diverged into separate directions with Mrs. Widmer close behind. As the armadillos bumped into bushes, shrubs, plants, and statues, the sound of shattering stone and glass echoed throughout the backyard. Mrs. Widmer then fixed her sight upon Irene running just across her feet and lifted the broom over her head in order to come down and strike her once and for all, but the handle got caught by her favorite bird house that was hanging just above her from a tree limb. The bird house, so thoughtfully decorated, went flying over her head and far down the yard where it came crashing down and shattered into pieces.

The commotion was so intense that it even stirred old Boomer, a basset hound from the house next door, to come and investigate. Boomer always looked tired and worn out, even for a basset hound. To drag himself up from his endless slumber was unusual. When at one time he'd chase squirrels and frolic in the yard fetching tennis balls, now he slept more than anything else. His bed was outside, just beneath the stairs leading to the deck of his owner's house. He stood up, shook himself as if to wake himself up, and casually walked over to the edge of his yard next to the garden wall in order to see what was going on.

Now growing frantic, running along in her nightgown and slippers, Mrs. Widmer tripped over an old stump and fell face flat into a muddy pool of rainwater only to have Willie run straight into her face with a terrible bump! Both were horrified and let out a terrible scream of fear and panic. Still watching from afar, Penni buried her head down under the doormat, unable to watch any longer. The chase resumed but now it was Mrs. Widmer running away from the armadillo pack! Round and round the precious plants and statues, tearing up the landscaping with woodchips and leaves flying through the air throughout the entire yard. Finally, while slipping and sliding along in the wet, muddy, and decimated garden she managed to make her way toward the house – the safety of the back door now within sight. She didn't see the last little armadillo, Mitch, crossing just in front of her path. She accidently stepped on his tail causing him to let out a terrible screeching scream! With this, she fell forward again, her arms stretched above her head, she fell swiftly into the muddy grass and the bird bath. The tub of the bird bath fell over spilling all the grungy, bird poop filled water down into her face before breaking into three large pieces. Mrs. Widmer spit out water from her lips, and moaned in complete horror at what had just happened, it was a disaster!

The armadillos quickly forgot about their friend Arnold, and the promise of a tasty treat, and scattered back the way they had come and off to home far down the road. Upon hearing the commotion, Arnold had poked his head up from inside the hole he had been digging. The first thing he saw was Boomer standing almost on top of him. The sight of Boomer's face startled Arnold intensely! He quickly sank back to complete his digging now more out of fear than hunger. His hole had now become an escape tunnel, and he quickly found himself having forged a way under the garden wall and into the yard next door. Boomer just quietly looked on in amazement. He even seemed to crack a smile at all the commotion, since anything that was this exciting had to be enjoyed, even if he was just watching.

Finally through to the other side of the wall, Arnold was safe, but he was now all on his own. As he reached the other side, he accidently moved a large stone out of his way and by doing so he dislodged a larger piece of the old brick garden wall which collapsed down behind him, blocking his way back into Mrs. Widmer's yard. But he didn't feel like taking his chances on going back there anyway, and he soon discovered exactly what it was that he had been sniffing after which made him forget about all the trouble he and his friends has caused. Before him was a seemingly giant pile of rotting wood, replete with a wide variety of slugs, ants, termites, and worms!

"Ah! LUNCH! And DINNER! Even BREAKFAST!" he exclaimed. It was the finest dining experience he could have ever dreamed of, and now it was all there for him to enjoy.

As Arnold lunged upon the woodpile, gobbling up slimy sluggish treat upon treat, he became so consumed with the feast that he didn't hear another door open, and then shut. Nor did he hear the two little voices which followed into the backyard.

"Andy look!" exclaimed Ellen as she spotted Arnold three layers high onto the wood pile.

"Wow, Ellen, it's an armadillo!" Andy responded and immediately began to race over for a closer look.

"Stop! Don't scare him," Ellen said, "He's so cute, and we don't want to hurt him."

The two kids approached slowly from behind. Sensing something, Arnold suddenly stopped eating and looked up, his mouth still dripping with worm guts and small ants and termites crawling up and down his little lips. Hearing nothing after a moment, he resumed his feast. Ellen and Andy moved quietly closer and closer until finally Andy could contain his enthusiasm no longer and blurted out,

"Hey! Who are you?"

Arnold stopped and turned around instantly. Fear began to race through him and for a moment he felt like running away. But he didn't know where to run. He couldn't see who had called him, even though they were only a few feet away. As Andy moved in to get a close look at him, the shadow Arnold saw took the shape of a giant human creature coming close! He tore off to his right as fast as he could. But within only a second or two, he ran right into a fence at the edge of the woodpile, and knocked himself out.

He woke to Ellen's soothing words of comfort and caring. The kids had taken Arnold into their fort tower which was attached to their swing set. They wrapped him in a blanket, and placed a thermometer in his mouth, proceeding to take his temperature. Arnold was in serious pain after eating so much, so fast. Combined with all the excitement and a severe blow to his head, he was now glad to be held and kept warm by Ellen and Andy's kind and caring words and actions. Ellen removed the thermometer and announced to Andy, "Ah good! His temperature is normal. For an armadillo anyway."

"What is normal for an armadillo, Ellen?" Andy inquired.

"I don't know, but I'm sure this is normal. He just looks normal now, don't you think?"

"I guess so. But I don't think I've ever seen an armadillo that was not normal." Andy responded. Then he proceeded to show Arnold his little red ball with which he sometimes played Jacks. He was moving it around, hoping Arnold would follow it with his eyes, but he just looked puzzled and more or less, straight ahead.

"He can't see that Andy. Armadillos don't see things well at all," Ellen said. Then, remembering how she recently had gotten new glasses, she wondered aloud, "Hey, maybe I can help him with a pair of glasses. I have my old ones that I can use!"

Arnold's Fort Tower Home

"Aren't those broken?" Andy asked.

"Yes, which is perfect! The smaller pieces will fit into some tiny frames! Will you make the frames Andy?"

"Sure!" Andy assured. "But wait, how do I make frames?"

"You'll figure it out. Stay here while I go get the glasses." Ellen said as she left. A few minutes later, she had the lenses, and Andy managed to secure the lenses to some little toy frames with some plastic zip ties he found in the garage. Together, the kids carefully placed them on

Arnold's nose. To Arnold, it was a whole new world which emerged! For the first time, the world was not a blur of shapeless, foggy images! Now he could clearly see the leaves on the trees, clouds in the sky, and best of all, the friendly smiles of his new best friends, Ellen and Andy. But there was something else magical about the glasses. Along with his new sight, came an ability to hear human words and speak them!

"Ah, wow!" an amazed Arnold blurted out! Ellen and Andy sat stunned at the articulate little armadillo.

"What did you say?" asked Andy.

"Who? Me?" replied Arnold.

"Yes, you. What did you just say? You said something, I mean, you really said something? Right?" Andy said, not believing his ears.

"Well, yes. I suppose I did say something," Arnold spoke after a moment of thought. "I've wanted to talk for such a long time! You have no idea how difficult it is to have so much to say and yet be unable to say it! I've wanted to tell others how beautiful the flowers smelled, or how nice the rain felt tapping on my back side. But I've never been able to form the words. But now, now I can say things! This is really incredible!"

"I'll say!" Ellen started, "No one at school will ever believe we have a talking armadillo! Say, what is your name?"

"I don't think I have a name." Arnold maintained.

"How about Arnold?" Andy proposed. "You look like an Arnold, I mean, if I ever knew an Arnold, I think he would look like you!"

The kids laughed and agreed that Arnold was indeed a wonderful name for an armadillo. Soon his tummy began to feel better as the kids told Arnold stories about their many adventures in and around their home. Arnold was very excited to have found two loving little people to care for and play with him. He was assured that he could eat as often as he wished, and that Ellen and Andy would return to see him every day after school. Arnold fell asleep that night in a nice warm bed Ellen has prepared for him, high above in the tree house in their backyard, overlooking Mrs. Widmer's devastated garden.

Chapter 2

The Windmills are Weakening

It was still fairly dark the next morning when Arnold woke to the sound of his stomach grumbling and rumbling again. He rose from his bed and proceeded over to the slide which was the only way an armadillo could get down from the top portion of the swing set, which the kids referred to as the Fort. He was very cautious as he neared the edge of the slide – it was a long way down! Arnold had forgotten about his glasses, so he was not able to see very clearly where the edge of the slippery slide began. He thought about just waiting for Ellen and Andy to come outside, but once again the smell of the food in and around the woodpile was overwhelming.

Slowly, he crept closer to the slide – his tiny toe nails scratching back and forth with his unease. He was right up on the edge of the green plastic slide and the clicking of his nails now sounded like someone typing fast on an old manual typewriter. Arnold's legs stretched in opposite directions, and he lost his footing as if he were walking on ice. The more he tried to regain himself, the more he ended up slipping! His stomach was no longer hungry, it was full of dread, as he knew he'd lost control and would soon be tumbling down the slide! One final slip and he was off, down the slide he went, going boldly where no armadillo had gone before! Arnold let out a panicked shriek as all four of his legs spread out to his sides. He was helpless to do anything, and worse still, he couldn't see where he was going! At last, he flew off the bottom edge of the slide and tumbled through the air like an acrobat, flipping and spinning around until finally coming to rest in a small pile of leaves and muddy grass.

Arnold was dazed and a bit confused as he picked himself up off the ground. But he soon thought about it, and as frightening as it was, he decided that he would like to try that again! He began sniffing around and allowed his nose to lead him over to a soft spot in the ground where he began to dig. He finally found some worms and grubs, but he had also found Ellen and Andy's vegetable garden. Without realizing it, Arnold quickly dug up much of the kid's vegetables and plants in pursuit of his tasty worms and grubs.

Arnold stopped as he heard shocked voices from above his head. He looked up, and could barely make out both Ellen and Andy who were saying things to him in a raised voice. It was then that Arnold realized he did not have his glasses, and he couldn't understand what they were saying. He could tell, however, by the tone of their voices that he was probably in trouble. Andy quickly picked Arnold up and began walking him back toward the swing set. Ellen retrieved his glasses from the fort, and placed them onto Arnold's face.

"Arnold! You can't go around digging up our yard or we won't be allowed to keep you!" Ellen lectured.

"You need to wear your glasses too. You weren't digging up the woodpile, that's in the opposite direction. You were digging up our garden!" Andy added.

"I'm sorry," Arnold said, "I didn't know you had a garden. What are vegetables?"

"They are people food, we grow them. Would you like to try some?" Andy asked.

"Sure!" Arnold answered, "I'm starving!"

Andy handed him a tomato and Arnold took a bite, only to spit it out. "Yuck!" Arnold said. I don't think I like people food. I prefer a nice fat, juicy worm!"

"That is so disgusting!" Ellen exclaimed. "Did you know worms have eight hearts, and they're slimy, and gross, and they move around and wiggle and... oh yuck!"

"I didn't know they had eight hearts," said Arnold. But he was not bothered; they still tasted good to him.

"Why don't we try some other kind of people food? How about bacon? Everyone loves bacon!" Andy said as he pulled a piece of bacon out from his coat pocket.

"Why do you have bacon in your pocket?" asked Ellen.

"I always hide an extra piece of bacon when we have it for breakfast. I eat it at school as a snack," Andy explained, and they both laughed. "Here Arnold, try this!" Andy held out a small piece of bacon for Arnold.

Arnold sniffed the bacon, which smelled wonderful. He took a bite and began to chew it. A moment later, he asked, "May I have more please?" Andy broke off another bit and offered it to Arnold who snapped it up rapidly. "A bit more please?"

"You're going to eat the whole thing?" asked Andy, surprised.

"Oh, yes please!" Arnold insisted, and took the entire strip of bacon from Andy's hand, ignoring the small bit he had planned to offer him. Ellen giggled as Arnold nearly swallowed the bacon whole! Andy sat there stunned and a bit sad that he had given Arnold all of his bacon, but, oh well. It was for his new armadillo friend and that was good enough. He began to laugh at how Arnold gulped down the bacon. But then, Arnold suddenly stopped eating. A terrifying look came over his face as if something was happening, but he didn't know what. Ellen and Andy leaned in closer to see what was wrong, when all of the sudden Arnold released an intensely long and loud burp!

"Wow!" Andy exclaimed while waving his hand in front of his nose! "That smells like really dirty bacon! Horrible!"

"That is the smell of bacon, worms, and grubs all mashed together. More like rotten pea soup!" Ellen added.

"Yum! I get to enjoy breakfast all over again!" Arnold proclaimed.

"Well, what do you say Arnold?" Ellen asked.

"More please?" replied Arnold.

"No, you need to mind your manners." Ellen insisted.

"Manners? What are manners and how would I go about minding them?" asked Arnold.

"Manners are how you do things. The proper way of doing things, or doing things, you know, properly." Ellen struggled.

"Just say 'excuse me', Arnold" added Andy.

"'Excuse me, Arnold'," Arnold replied. The kids laughed, and Arnold felt a little hurt that he didn't understand.

"After you burp, for example," Ellen began, "you have to say 'excuse me' to show others that you're sorry for making such a yucky noise. You're kind of like, saying you're sorry for being gross and inconsiderate."

"Yeah," Andy added, "Like when you eat, there are table manners. You keep your napkin on your lap, your elbows off the table, and your mouth closed when you chew. But I sort of disagree with that one. It's a lot easier to chew without worrying about keeping your mouth closed."

"Why do you keep your mouth closed?" asked Arnold.

"So I don't have to see his 'see-food'!" replied Ellen giving Andy a little smirk.

"And what is a napkin?" asked Arnold.

"I can see this is going to take a little time," said Ellen. "Let's go over things when we get back from school. In the meantime, don't leave our yard for any reason. Andy will get you a nice supply of worms and grubs for lunch, and we'll be back and have a nice supper."

"Here Arnold, you can read this book while we're at school." Andy said as he placed down a graphic novel featuring the life of King Arthur and his Knights of the Round Table. "It is all about manners, and chivalry, and how to be a noble hero!" The kids then headed off to school.

Arnold looked carefully at the book when it occurred to him that despite his new glasses and the magical abilities they seemed to provide, he could not read a single word. But thankfully for Arnold, the book was almost entirely composed of illustrations. Arnold spent the day studying the pages of the book, and thinking about the idea of manners and helping others. The knights pictured in the book seemed not all that different than himself. They were clothed in shining armor, which seemed similar to his own thick plating on his back and head. He also learned about how the knights used lances and swords in battle in order to save and protect the fair maiden and princess. This much he was able to discern from the pictures. By mid-morning Arnold grew very hungry again and ate the food Andy had left for him. He then grew very tired, took off his glasses, and settled down for a nice long nap.

Meanwhile, on the other side of the old garden wall, Mrs. Widmer's backyard was full of activity. Several men were working throughout the day to repair and reconstruct Mrs. Widmer's once gorgeous garden. The sound of shovels pushing against stones and the smell of fresh woodchips filled the cool spring air. A large stainless steel gazing ball, birdbath, and a few new garden gnomes accompanied the new landscaping. A striking miniature windmill standing about five feet tall, just like one you might find at a miniature golf course, topped it all off. By lunchtime, Mrs. Widmer was able to finally settle down with Penni and a nice warm cup of tea amongst the petunias and marigolds of her tranquil bit of paradise. The hole under the garden wall had been sealed, and she felt quite satisfied that nothing more could possible go wrong. Penni let out a cute little bark, and Mrs. Widmer bent over to her with a delicate little doggie treat, all was right with her world.

Penni's sharp little bark startled Arnold from his sleep. Since Armadillos don't hear very well, he listened carefully for a moment to try to make sense of the sound. Penni barked again, as she was prone to do while begging for additional doggie treats. But to Arnold, the sound was concerning and unusual. Penni's barks soon grew into high-pitched moans as she wined and cried in order to convince Mrs. Widmer to feed her more treats. Mrs. Widmer was enjoying the game, as she always did, admiring her cute little Yorkie and every so often giving in to her pitiful cries.

It was clear to Arnold that something terrible had happened to Penni. He peered through the plastic toy telescope attached to the side of the tree house, and gazed into Mrs. Widmer's backyard to investigate. But Arnold was very disappointed in that he couldn't see much at all through the telescope, not realizing that he had once again forgotten to put on his glasses. He decided that Penni's cries were cries for help, and that she was in terrible danger. There was only one thing he could do. Remembering the book, he started toward the slide and quickly flew into action!

Arnold ran over toward the garden wall under which he could pass into Mrs. Widmer's yard once again, but he found it sealed by rocks, gravel, and dirt. "To dig through that would take forever!" he thought. Just then, he remembered the old dog from next door. He moved down the fence of the backyard and found a narrow opening underneath, then managed to squeeze through into the Baker's backyard next door. Boomer was an old basset hound dog, the kind that hunters would sometimes use to chase and tree raccoons. But Boomer was well past his prime, and spent most of his time sleeping.

Boomer seemed to have a permanent "Do not disturb" sign for a dog tag, and so Arnold approached him with great caution. Still without his glasses, Arnold naturally relied on his sense of smell to find Boomer. But when he got close, he simply couldn't see well enough to avoid knocking over a small table on which were some shrubbery clippers, gloves, and a small silver shovel whose handle had broken off. The noise seemed loud enough to wake the entire neighborhood! Boomer moaned and seemed to find just enough energy to lift an eyelid. To his surprise he saw an armadillo standing right in front of him. In the old days, this would have been the chasing opportunity of a lifetime! But now, it was an unpleasant nuisance.

"Boomer?" Arnold asked in a quiet voice. Boomer just stared at him wishing he would simply go away and let him fall back to sleep in peace. "Boomer?" Arnold inquired once more. This time Boomer took a deep breath, but still said nothing. "Boomer!" shouted Arnold.

"What!" An annoyed Boomer finally responded in his low baritone voice.

"We need to rescue Penni, she's in terrible trouble!" Arnold explained.

"Trouble?" replied Boomer, as if he didn't even know what the word meant. He did, of course, but the fact was that he didn't care about the neighbor's dog, much less the armadillo standing in front of him. His question was his way of trying to play dumb in order to get Arnold to leave.

"Yes! I am like a brave knight, and I must save the poor maiden. She has been calling for assistance now all afternoon, and we must go and help her. I cannot get under the wall on my own, I need your help to carry me up and over the fence in your backyard and around into the jungle where Penni is being held against her will. We haven't much time, and I am prepared to do battle and mind my manners in order to rescue her from the clutches of whatever evil monster has placed her at his mercy!" Arnold finally finished and was out of breath, huffing and puffing with excitement, perhaps he also needed some convincing.

"Oh," Boomer replied, his deep and low voice indicating that he was less than excited about the prospect of waking up, much less of helping this armadillo. He closed his eyes, took a deep sigh, and began to fall back to sleep.

"Please Boomer! I cannot do this on my own!" Arnold continued. Boomer forced himself to open his eyes once more and began to glare at Arnold. "If we succeed we will be the most famous and noble knights of the entire neighborhood! We will have made up for the mess we made of Mrs. Widmer's jungle and have earned the prestigious titles of being knights. I will be given a sword and the King will knight me. And you will be given a sash and be given some title as well, which I am sure will be really great." Arnold went on for a few more minutes, trying to reason with Boomer and get him to join his crusade to rescue Penni. But he finally ran out of breath, and fell to the ground exhausted from the workout of talking and pacing around in front of the tired old dog.

"Oh," Boomer replied once more, closed his eyes and began to fall back to sleep. But then, Arnold suddenly remembered something.

"Boomer?" he whispered softly into Boomer's ear. "There will be bacon!" Boomer's eyes opened immediately. The thought of food always aroused his interest, but meat in general was his soft spot, a temptation he couldn't resist.

"Bacon?" asked Boomer.

"Bacon," smiled Arnold. "Andy has lots of bacon in the morning, and he shared it with me. I will make sure you have two handfuls of warm, crispy bacon!" Arnold promised. The thought of bacon made Boomer salivate as if he was descended from one of Pavlov's famous dogs, and he had just heard the dinner bell.

"What's this plan again?" Boomer asked. Arnold began to review the rescue plan once more with Boomer. As he was explaining, Arnold grabbed several of the items that had fallen from the table. He managed to fashion a saddle out of the old garden gloves, and a shield out of the little garden shovel. He also found a long, straight stick he would use as a lance, just like the knights in the book Andy had left for him. He fashioned a handle, and prepared Boomer for the ride over the fence, and to the rescue.

"You know how to get there, don't you?" Asked Arnold.

"I used to sneak over there all the time when I was little to bury bones!" Boomer said, somewhat annoyed at the question. "I know where to go."

"Bury bones?" Arnold asked. He imagined Boomer killing another small animal, eating it for supper, and then hiding the evidence of his crime by burying the bones in Mrs. Widmer's jungle, how terrible. He would have to watch his step around Boomer. But in reality, Boomer was referring to the bones he used to get from his owner, Mr. Baker, who would give him the center bone from the prime rib he would have for supper. In any case, Arnold leapt onto Boomers back, and they began their gallant rescue attempt in earnest.

Boomer was quite old and moved very slowly across his backyard toward the fence. Arnold realized that he could have walked much faster, and that he probably could get over the fence by himself without much difficulty. But he was glad to have Boomer with him just that same. For who knows what kind of danger he would have to face in order to save little Penni from the evil that had been causing her cries! Eventually, Boomer made it to the fence. It was an old wooden fence that consisted of several posts and two beams connected across between each of them. It was wide open below the beams, any creature could have walked on through. Boomer did, but without thought to Arnold on his back. Slam!

"Ouch!" cried Arnold as his head smacked up against the lower beam of the fence. "Watch where you're going brave Boomer!" Arnold shouted.

"Huh?" responded Boomer, not sure why he was being scolded but also appreciating that he was being called brave. He never thought of himself as brave, only hungry and tired. The duo pressed onward toward Mrs. Widmer's backyard, with Boomer taking the long way around toward the front of her house where the gate was located. But upon reaching the gate they found it closed.

"Hum," moaned Boomer. "I guess we can't get in. Do I still get bacon?" Boomer asked.

"No!" Arnold commanded. "Not until I rescue the maiden in distress!" Arnold tried to look around for another way into the backyard, but he couldn't see much at all without his glasses, of course, so he invented a new plan.

"We will bypass this gateway and try entering up that shaft attached to the house." The shaft was actually a rain gutter. "We will then climb out onto the back porch rooftop, where we will have an unobstructed view of the entire jungle area. Once we locate the damsel Penni, you will leap down from the roof, I on your back, and we shall ride off together with her and enjoy bacon for dinner as hero's and with all the proper manners! This will prove my worthiness to be Ellen and Andy's friend and pet." Arnold's plan was based on pure imagination, but it sounded quite inspirational nonetheless.

"Hum. Maybe I could just push the door open with my nose." Boomer said as he moved toward the gate and began to push. Sure enough, it opened with ease.

"Yeah. That could work too I suppose" retorted Arnold, somewhat embarrassed. As they walked around the corner, Arnold ordered Boomer to stop. He squinted hard, trying to see something large on the opposite side of the yard. He quickly concluded that it was a giant monster, with four arms waving in the air! This must be what was causing Penni's distress! Just then he heard Penni's desperate bark, as if she were calling for Arnold to come rescue her.

"It's a giant monster, Boomer!" Arnold announced as he began to scramble to place his lance along his side in preparation for an attack!

"Monster?" Boomer asked as he also began to squint. The old dog's eye sight was not what it used to be, but he did have an excellent sense of smell to detect strangers (and food,) and he didn't smell anything other than the aroma of beautiful flowers.

"Prepare to charge, Boomer!" Arnold commanded.

"Charge?" replied Boomer, surprised and a bit confused.

"Now Boomer! Run! Attack the monster and I'll save the maiden Penni from its hideous clutches!" Arnold had never felt so brave and honorable, but Boomer wasn't the kind of dog that enjoyed running anymore. After standing still for a moment, Arnold grew impatient. "Bacon! Bacon Boomer! For the bacon!" Boomer thought about it, and decided that even though he doubted there was a monster, he'd indulge Arnold one last time if it meant a tasty bacon reward. The old dog slowly began to walk toward the monster. His walk soon became a jog, and then slowly built up into a weak run. His old bones and muscles were giving all they could, and Arnold lowered himself on Boomer's back, with his lance poised to deal the deadly blow!

Boomer kept running, until several feet before reaching their target when he finally realized that it was not a monster that they were attacking, it was a windmill. Boomer came to a sudden stop, but Arnold kept going. He was flung forward into the air toward the windmill. Arnold's lance pierced one of the windmill's blades to the sound of Arnold's frantic scream! The lance ended up lodged into the blade, with Arnold holding onto it for dear life. The windmill continued to turn and took Arnold for a ride up and down, round and round. Now, it was Arnold who was shouting for help!

Penni had been watching the commotion from the back door window, and continued to bark. Boomer looked embarrassed, and shook his head thinking about the fact that he'd probably not be eating any bacon after all. Finally, Mrs. Widmer approached the back door and looked out over her beautiful garden to notice an armadillo hanging from a stick lodged into her windmill. For once, Mrs. Widmer was speechless, although she did let out an exasperated scream, which caught the attention of Andy as he was returning home from school.

Andy ran into the backyard garden, and noticed Arnold instantly. It was a strange sight indeed to see the armadillo swinging around and around on a windmill! He quickly ran over and rescued Arnold. He took both Arnold and Boomer back home, and gave Boomer a piece of bacon he had saved. He then scolded Arnold, "You shouldn't spend your time tilting at windmills!"

Chapter 3

The Canterbury Park Tales

The weekend couldn't come fast enough for Arnold. He would finally be spending some significant time with his new friends, Ellen and Andy, who were going to take him to the neighborhood park. Actually, the kids had never been there before, and weren't even sure the park really existed. It was something their father had told them about quite some time ago, but they never got around to actually going. They knew the basic direction; turn left on Oak Street, then right on Elm, and then follow that road as it twists and turns throughout the neighborhood until you come to Canterbury Street. Somewhere along Canterbury Street was supposed to be Canterbury Park. Legend had it that there were tire swings, slides, a giant jungle gym, and spooky tunnels which ran under the ground. It was going to be exciting, especially if they actually did find Canterbury Park.

"Are you ready to go Arnold?" Ellen asked as she climbed into the covered fort-tower of their swing set, where Arnold slept in order to keep him safe at night.

Arnold quickly put on his glasses and answered, "Oh yes! To the park we go!" He was so excited to get going that he leaped over his bed, dashed past Ellen and jumped onto the slide and zoomed down at high speed! He went so fast, that he actually flew off the end of the slide back up into the air as if he was flying off the end of a giant ski jump! Fortunately, Andy was there to catch him! Andy hugged Arnold, laughed and said, "You're one crazy Armadillo Arnold!"

"Thank you for catching me, Andy. But I am so excited about going to the park today" said Arnold.

"Well, we need to pack lunch, it's a long way to the park. If we even find it" Andy warned.

"What would you like to eat for lunch, Arnold?" asked Ellen.

"I don't know. Perhaps whatever you're having?" replied Arnold, remembering how tasty human food had been.

"Well, we're having ham sandwiches. Andy should be able to dig up some grubs and worms for you."

"Oh." Arnold said, rather dejected. "I guess that will be ok."

"I have an idea for a special sandwich for you Arnold," said Andy sensing his disappointment, "Wait here."

Several minutes later Andy returned from the house with their lunch bags and announced proudly, "Arnold! I made you a very special vegemite sandwich! Perfect for any armadillo!"

Arnold took a sniff from his brown lunch sac, and smiled, it smelled absolutely delectable. He was ready for lunch already!

"Okay!" announced Ellen, "Let's get going, we have a very long walk."

The three friends slowly made their way out to the front of the house, loaded Arnold up into their little red toy wagon, and began their journey down the sidewalk. After several minutes of silence, it occurred to Ellen that in order to help pass the time, they could each tell a story to one another. Ellen explained her idea to Andy and Arnold.

"Great idea Ellen!" Andy replied. "I have a great one to start!"

Arnold perked up and stirred in the wagon, anxious to hear the story. As they continued their walk, Andy began his tale.

Andy's Tale

One day while out in the woods, running fast
Three young boys racing so not to be last
Came across a little house in a glade.
Thirsty, they hoped they'd find some lemon-aid
They knocked on the door but no one was home
Looked all around and were surely alone
So they went inside to see what was there
Just like Goldilocks without the three bears
Then there on the table in a huge bowl

More chocolate pudding than ten boys could hold!
Their hungry jaws fell straight onto the floor
For their wildest dreams couldn't dream more!
And just as they leapt to take their first bite
One boy called out, "Wait! This just isn't right!
Why waste the chance at living out a dream
When all we'd need is some lovely whipped cream!
That and a cherry placed right on the top!
Then we could eat it all, every last drop!"
So it was suggested that one should leave
Run into to town and the goodies retrieve.
They quickly drew lots to see who would go
And who'd remain to keep watch on the bowl.
The youngest drew short, so off then he went
The other two stayed, and sat on the bench.
It wasn't long after the third had gone
The oldest declared that something was wrong
"Why should we have to split this treat by three?
When the two of us can quite easily
Take the whip cream and cherries from his arms
And lock him outside where he'll do us no harm.
Then we'll have all the pudding for ourselves
As well as cream and cherries to indulge!"
And straight away the second kid agreed
And they spent all their time plotting the deed.

Meanwhile the youngest had gone to the town
When once there a bright idea he found.
He'd buy something that would leave them so sick
They'd never know it was all a great trick!

He'd soak the cherries in a sickly brew
They'd fall over in pain, their faces blue
Then he'd be free to indulge in a feast
Of chocolate pudding with a creamy treat!
He'd eat it all, every last chocolate drop
For nothing could ruin his fool proof plot!
So he took the cherries, soaking them good
And confidently set off for the woods.
When he arrived it didn't take him long
To sense that something was terribly wrong
The older two jumped him, knocking him down
And with the sweet toppings swung fast around
They ran for the house and secured the lock
Just in time to make safe what they got
They wasted no time and they took no heed
Entirely consumed with selfish greed
They added the cream to the pudding sweet
And topped it all off with the cherry treat.
They couldn't find forks and they had no spoons
So they dove right in with all they could use
Submerging their heads, mouths open instead
The cherries went first, and then came the dread.
Their stomachs churned as it started back up
Just like a volcano poised to erupt
Horrid hot liquid flew like a comet
Blasting the room, soaking it with vomit.
The stench so pungent, no window ajar,
The whole place loaded with rotting thick barf
They fell to the floor still riving in pain
Their shouting and pleas for mercy in vain

They rolled around on the vomit laced floor
'til they just couldn't throw up any more.
(The end of Andy's Tale)

"Andy that is probably the most disgusting story I've ever heard in my life!" Ellen scolded, looking a little sick to her stomach. "I don't think I even want to eat lunch now!"

"Then can I have your pudding cup?" Andy smiled. But even Arnold was holding his nose; he wasn't feeling too good either.

"That was a very interesting story, Andy." Said Arnold. "Right up until the end, I was really getting hungry! But I don't understand why they stopped each other from eating the pudding. Why didn't they share it in the first place?" he asked.

"That's the point, Arnold." Andy answered. "They were greedy, and the moral of the story is that you should share things. Especially when there is more than enough to go around."

"I see." Said Arnold. Just then, they heard a loud, moaning meow coming from some bushes nearby.

"What was that?" asked Andy.

"Sounds like a cat!" answered Arnold, confidently. He knew the various sounds of other animals well.

"If it's a cat, it sounds like it's in pain!" said Ellen, sympathetically.

"Meeeeoooooowww!!!" The cry came once again.

"It sounds... desperate." Ellen said, growing very concerned. They stopped and Ellen called out toward the bushes. "Hello? Here kitty, here!" Ellen gently called, bending down close to the ground near the edge of the bush. A regal looking cat quickly ran out toward Ellen's outstretched hand, and sniffed.

"Meow!" the cat said, happy to see someone. But he shifted around as if he had lost something important and was trying to figure out what to do about finding it.

"Awe, what's the matter kitty?" Ellen asked.

"I've lost my love," he answered. "I've lost her forever!"

"What is your name?" Ellen asked.

"Otto," he said.

"Otto. It's nice to meet you. My name is Ellen, this is my brother Andy, and our friend Arnold."

"Your friend? He's ah, well, he's an Armadillo!" Otto said.

"Yeah," replied Andy, "he is an Armadillo. And he's an awesome armadillo!"

"Thanks!" Arnold said, smiling. "Perhaps we can help you, Otto."

"Have you seen my love? She's a beautiful princess. Her name is Gisele. We were to meet here to go off and live happily ever after, but she never showed up." Otto explained.

"No, we haven't seen anyone" answered Andy.

"We're heading to Canterbury Park. Would you like to come with us? Ellen offered. Maybe Gisele went there too.

"I do not think she will be at the park. I have a feeling her family may have moved and taken her with them, I may never see her again." Otto said feeling very sad.

"That's terrible," cried Arnold. "I was feeling sick to my stomach, now I'm feeling sad in my chest"

"We need another story! I know one that was even grosser!" Andy began.

"No!" Ellen and Arnold both interrupted, then all three laughed.

"It's my turn anyway." Ellen started.

"We're telling stories to help pass the time along our trip, Otto." Explained Arnold.

"I see. Well, I don't really know any stories." Otto replied.

"That's okay," said Arnold, "I don't know any either. And it's Ellen's turn anyway."

Yes, it's my turn, so now I'll begin." Said Ellen, and as they all resumed slowly making their way down the sidewalk, pulling Arnold and Otto in the red wagon, she began to tell her tale.

Ellen's Tale

"What's black and white, black and white, black and white?
A penguin rolling down a hill in fright!
The princess giggled and laughed at the thought
That an out of control penguin had brought.
She imagined his panic and his scream
And how absolutely absurd it seemed.
But such were the stories of the young King
Told to her to make sure she was laughing.
He told them in order to see her smile
Before he'd have to leave for a while.
He'd never known a laugh so wonderful
Or eyes so alive, blue and beautiful.
But then one day, her family moved away

And they promised to write every day.
He wrote jokes to her, recalling her laugh
She wrote back to him that she'd soon be back.
But then one day the King's mother found one
Of the love letters and all came undone.
Fearing her son had decided to leave
And marry this girl she had never seen
She took pen to his paper and altered
His words until the girl's love would falter.
Instead of saying, "her laugh was so sweet"
She wrote that her, "Breath smelled like dirty feet."
And she never held a place in his heart
'cause the perfume she wore stunk like a fart.
The thought she sang like a beautiful bird
Was a thought he now found wholly absurd!
Her voice was a screeching headache of hurt
And her fingernails were packed full of dirt.
She wrote that her hair felt like barbed wire,
Her skin as rough as an old used tire.
And finally he hoped she'd just disappear
And how he'd never even shed a tear.
So his mother sent the letter that day
Convinced it would keep that princess away

But when she read it, she didn't believe
He'd ever betray her and so deceive.
She set out to find him and learn the truth
Before she'd give up, she'd demand proof!
She set sail for his kingdom the next day
But a storm came and blew the ship away

Far from her home and his, she now survived
As a servant for a family of five.
All alone, it didn't take her too long
Before all the guys were drawn to her song.
The first man tempted her with his great wealth,
A second with his bravery, skill, and health.
A third man used power and influence
But none of them were able to convince
her to give up on the one in her heart,
The King she had known and loved from the start.
Then one day after many months had past,
She heard there was a visitor at last.
Someone who had been searching far and near
For a certain princess he loved so dear.
His Dad once told him, "When stuck in a rut,
Never, never, never, never give up!"
So when he heard, he knew that it must be
His darling princess who turned away three!
For his love shone as brightly as the sun
And that's why, in her heart, she knew he'd come.
Then he told her a joke, to hear her laugh,
About how a penguin ate a giraffe.
So remember, when the going gets rough
Be patient and true – that will be enough.
For all good things come to those who will wait
And learn to embrace the strange twists of fate.

(The end of Ellen's Tale)

"That was a wonderful story, Ellen!" announced Arnold, proudly.

"A nice story" said Otto, "I'm feeling a little better now, thank you!"

"Hey, look!" Andy cried, "There's the park! It is real after all!" Just down the road was a clearing in the neighborhood, just in front of the forest, which extended as far as anyone knew. The park was large and had several slides, swings, and tennis courts, as well as an enormous field on which many kids were playing tag and football. There were also many dogs, cats, birds, squirrels, and yes, even a few armadillos there, all playing various games and having a great time.

Arnold was amazed at all the activities, and was very grateful to his new friends for pulling the little red wagon all the way to the park. He and Otto got off the wagon and ran over toward the edge of the woods to meet some of the other animals. The squirrels were a little wary of Otto at first, and Otto was a little wary of the dogs! But Arnold spent time introducing himself and Otto to the other animals, and even a couple of the children Ellen and Andy brought over to meet him. None of the kids had ever seen a real, talking armadillo before! His magical glasses not only made him see the world more clearly, but they also helped to reveal one of his most wonderful qualities, his ability to make new friends and help others feel good about themselves and each other.

Otto had been alone for a long time, so when Ellen and Andy offered him a place to stay he accepted. Otto was a very intelligent cat, he had survived on his own for most of his life, and he never gave up hope that his Gisele would someday return to him.

After several hours of playing at Canterbury Park, the kids packed up the wagon and headed back home. It was Arnold's turn to tell a story, but the only story he could think of was one about a lonely armadillo who one day found the greatest friends he could ever imagine.

Chapter 4

The Hound of the Baker's

The terrible screaming shattered the quiet still of the night. Even Arnold, who is a little hard of hearing, woke suddenly from his bed atop the swing set's Fort tower where he had been sharing his room with Otto, his new friend who decided to stay with Ellen and Andy following their trip to Canterbury Park. The screaming was from an animal but it was more of a desperate moaning as if it was in great pain. When Arnold woke, he called for Otto to ask him what was happening. But Otto was not in his bed. A worried Arnold began to look around frantically for his friend.

"Otto!" Arnold called in a whisper. Trying hard to stay quiet while shouting is not an easy thing for an Armadillo, but he received no answer. Arnold's mind began to move quickly with worry and panic as he thought that perhaps the painful shrieking was actually coming from Otto, who may have been injured and was now suffering and calling for help. Arnold was preparing to make his way toward and down the slide and into the yard in order to investigate further, but he was fighting his own fear – facing a terrifying unknown. But just as Arnold made up his mind to slide down into action, he remembered he didn't have his glasses on. He walked over to the little table where he kept them – and after putting them on he heard a sharp yet light voice, which seemed to come from nowhere.

Otto

"My dear Arnold, don't leave the fort."

"Otto? Is that you?" Arnold asked to the empty room. "Where are you?"

"Shhh, Arnold. Come here." The voice seemed to be coming from the roof, which was a canopy, draped over a wooden beam forming a gable. But Arnold could not climb to the rooftop. So he made his way toward the edge of the fort where his specially built ladder rested against the floor.

He walked out and looked up toward the canopy roof where he saw Otto, sitting calmly and majestically atop the fort. "What are you doing up there?" called Arnold.

"Ah, Arnold. It's good to see you. I have been up here for most of the night. From here I can see the entire neighborhood." Otto seemed in complete control despite the terrible situation occurring just a short distance away.

"What's going on?" asked Arnold, knowing that a cats eyes are much more sensitive and able to see well in the dark, he hoped Otto could explain who or what was making the shrieking noises.

"I'm not sure." Otto suddenly slid down the canopy, flipping down at the edge and landing square on his feet just in front of where Arnold was standing. "But it's bad, Arnold."

"What are we going to do?" asked Arnold, worried for whoever was suffering nearby.

"It is coming from next door, the Baker's" Otto said confidently yet gravely. "I'm afraid there is nothing much we can do."

"But, shouldn't we go and investigate?" asked Arnold.

"That would be unwise, my dear Arnold. There is obvious danger, and far too many dangerous creatures are out and about at night around here. We will wait until morning to begin our investigation."

But it was a restless night for Arnold as the moaning and shrieking continued all through the night.

The next morning Arnold was still sleeping when Otto suddenly roused him.

"We have a visitor!" Otto said excitedly. Arnold quickly

got up and rushed to the edge of the fort. Looking down he could see a large Maine Coon cat looking around the yard as if he was lost.

Finally, the cat spotted Otto and Arnold looking down and then asked, "May I speak with you?"

Otto spoke to Arnold in a soft tone, "Tell him to come on up." Arnold was not sure why Otto didn't just tell him himself, but he did so and the Maine Coon slowly made his way up the ramp and ladder and into the fort. Otto had quickly placed himself across the floor, into a corner so as to command the entire room. The Maine Coon looked nervous and on edge as he approached Arnold and Otto.

"Pleased to meet you!" Arnold began. "My name is Arnold, and this is Otto. Who are you?"

"My name is Henry, I just moved into the Baker's home next door."

"Ah, that wasn't you we heard last night was it?" Arnold asked.

"No, no, I don't know what that was, but I was up all night panicking about it. I was hoping you would know what was going on to cause such a terrible noise!" Although he was a large cat, it was clear that Henry was very domesticated and had not much experience with the wild. He looked tired, and his eyes were very large and gentle. On the other hand, Otto had spent most of his life in the wild before finding an owner who took him in. Through his experience Otto had learned all there was about humans as well as famous stories and mysteries. Because of this, Otto was intrigued. Since coming back home to live with Arnold, Ellen and Andy, he had become rather bored. There was nothing like a good mystery to pique Otto's senses! This was proving to be a very exciting day for him, although both Henry and Arnold felt very uneasy.

"When exactly did you move in?" Otto inquired.

"Two days ago, Mr. Baker likes to keep me inside. But after last night, I had to come out and find out." Henry suddenly stopped himself.

"Find out what, exactly?" asked Otto, but Henry looked down and didn't say a word. "If you came all this way for help, don't hold anything back. If you wish to keep your secrets, then go home!" Otto snapped.

"Otto! Be nice." Said Arnold, trying to make Henry feel better. "It's been a long night, perhaps you'd like some milk?" Arnold offered Henry.

"Thank you," said Henry, "I will tell you all that I've heard, but I warn you, it is a frightening story."

"You must tell me every detail if I am to be of service to you." Otto commanded. His poise was like a statue. He was confident and excited, yet reserved and in complete control.

"It began months ago, while I was still living with my previous owner down the street. His grandchildren would stay over often and he would tell them stories at night about a great hound dog, which roamed around the neighborhood when he was a little boy. The hound lived at the Baker's house, and he was a giant hound at least three times larger than any dog he'd ever seen! He could run faster than any animal or human and loved chasing them and attacking anyone who would dare to come near his

50

master's backyard.

One night, the old hound lost his sense of direction and was hit by a car and killed. After that, all the animals and little children were relieved that the vicious hound would bother them no more. But then, on the first full moon, the ghost of that hound dog appeared and savagely attacked a wild raccoon, ripping his throat out and was then seen standing proudly over the body until the moonlight disappeared late in the night. The legend says that he glowed in the night, and that he could sense you from a mile away. He would then lay and wait until you came close enough. Then, without warning, he would jump upon you, rip your throat out, and eat your guts for his supper.

Even now, years later, it is said that screams could still be heard on those dark, quiet nights as that was when the ghost hound still appears to take his revenge on anyone who gets too close to his master's yard, the old Baker house. I am convinced that that was what caused the screaming and terrorizing noises last night! And now, I am living there and I am in fear of my life!"

As Henry concluded his story, Arnold was wide-eyed, even for an Armadillo. He was trembling and looked toward Otto who hadn't moved a muscle. His ears had been perked up for listening, and now they finally relaxed.

"And you believe this hound caused the commotion last night?" Otto asked sternly.

"I don't know. Maybe," was all Henry could answer.

"Well, there is definitely something mysterious going on!" Arnold chimed in, feeling confident in his conclusion.

"And I'm convinced the hound is responsible. But what are we going to do about it?" Arnold asked, turning to Otto.

"*We?*" asked Otto. "More like *you.*"

"Me?" a stunned Arnold gasped.

"Yes, you will accompany Henry back to the Baker's. I have many other pressing things I should need to finish before concerning myself with this affair. Go gather some clues from around the backyard. Write down everything, and plan to spend the night with Henry." Otto concluded his instructions.

"But I am an indoor cat, Otto. Arnold won't be allowed to come inside." Said Henry.

"Yes, yes, that's right!" said Arnold excitedly, hoping this might be a way out of having to spend the night among the scary happenings of the Baker's. He quickly added, "Well, I guess that plan won't work, so I better plan on..."

Otto interrupted, "You will stay night out on the back patio. But do stay far from that old hound dog. One never knows."

"Boomer?" Arnold asked. "You don't think old Boomer is *the* hound, do you?" But Otto just stared at Arnold, expecting him to go at once and search for clues.

"Say," asked Henry, "How do you get down from here, Arnold? You don't climb well do you?"

"The slide!" Arnold announced as he ran over to the top edge of the slide. "It's a lot of fun, and makes for a quick exit! Wanna try?"

Henry began looking down from the top, and he didn't see how a slide would be anything near fun. "No, I'm not much of a slider." But no sooner did he utter those words than did Arnold push him onto the top of the slippery slope, and down Henry flew! His Maine Coon fur quickly picked up enough static electricity to make every hair on his body stick straight up. Or it could have been because he was scared to death as he flew down the slide at high speed, his legs spread out far and wide as he slid down on his tummy like a rocket! But like all good cats, after he flew off the edge he quickly managed to land on his feet. Henry took a deep breath and felt relieved. Then, just as he turned around to see where he had just come from, he saw Arnold also flying down the slide and heading right at him, tail end first!

"Ahhhh!" shouted Henry, but it was too late. Arnold's rear end landed right on top of Henry's head. They were a sight indeed as Arnold struggled to put his glasses back onto his head, while Henry was laid out cold, it looked as though Arnold was riding on top of a Maine Coon horse!

Otto peered down from the top of the slide and shook his head. Then he climbed back up to the top of the canopy and perched himself in his favorite thinking spot overlooking the backyard.

It was then that Ellen and Andy happened to come out to greet them.

"Good morning, Arnold," greeted Ellen, who was all smiles.

"We're going to the aquarium today!" shouted Andy in excitement. "I wish we could take you, but I don't think they would want an armadillo scaring away all the fish."

"And Otters," Ellen added.

"Hey, it's too bad Otto isn't an otter, then he'd be Otto the otter!" Andy said, and they all laughed.

"Who is your new friend?" asked Ellen.

Arnold introduced Henry just as he was coming around. "He lives next door with the Baker's. Do you know much about Mr. Baker?" Arnold began his investigation in to the mystery.

"A little." Ellen replied. "Andy and I used to go visit him and his wife in the summer time."

"Yeah, we would play with Boomer and sit on their back porch with them and watch TV." Andy added. "They are nice people."

"Well, you behave today and have fun with your new friend." Ellen said as they headed off to the aquarium for the day. Arnold pulled out his note pad and jotted down the fact that Ellen and Andy knew Mr. Baker and his wife, and they were nice people. Then Henry and Arnold made their way into the Baker's backyard in order to gather more clues.

Just past the fence, Arnold discovered a Starburst wrapper! He sniffed it and was immediately excited! "Wow, this smells so incredible!" Arnold looked up with the little yellow wrapper now stuck to his nose as if it were a vacuum.

"It is a piece of candy. That stuff tastes terrible!" Henry replied.

"Terrible? Oh no, this is simply fantastically scrumptious!" Arnold shouted, almost panting with joy. "I just love human food! Especially candy!"

"So, what you're saying is that some humans have been around here recently?" Henry asked.

After thinking about it, it sounded like a very reasonable conclusion, so Arnold took credit saying, "Yes. That is exactly what this means!" But Henry remained skeptical.

They moved further across the backyard closer to the house. Off to the side they noticed Boomer, laying down in the shade next to his water bowl, as usual. Boomer had been so quiet all this time that Henry didn't even realize a dog lived there.

"The hound!" said Henry in a surprised tone.

"No. I mean, yes. Well, yes he's a hound, but no, he's not *the* hound," Arnold fumbled his words as he tried to explain. He told Henry that boomer was simply a grumpy old dog, who more or less ate bacon and slept. But Henry was still very suspicious
and crept closer to Boomer. He walked up close in order to get a good look. Arnold finally freed the Starburst wrapper from his nose and ran to catch up with Henry.

"I got it off!" Arnold shouted excitedly.

"Shhh!" cried Henry, "You'll wake him!" But it was too late. Boomer slowly opened his eyes and took in a deep breath as if he was annoyed at the interruption. His cheek slapped like a snare drum as he exhaled.

"Not again," Boomer lamented. "What are you doing here?" he asked.

Henry was so frightened that he couldn't say a word – he just froze. But Arnold replied instantly, "We're looking in to whoever ate candy here recently.

Have you seen anyone?" Arnold asked.

"No," Boomer replied. "Do you have any bacon?" he asked.

"No. Sorry," Arnold answered.

Disappointed, Boomer closed his eyes and instantly fell back to sleep. Arnold quickly took more notes in his notepad
about the candy wrapper. He hoped they would find more, particularly some with candy still left inside it!

"Psst! Boomer," Arnold whispered loudly into the old dog's ear waking him up once again. This time, Boomer simply opened his eyes but was too tired to raise his head. He didn't say anything he just gave a long protracted sigh.

"Boomer, did you hear or see anything here last night? Anything out of the ordinary?" Arnold asked.

Boomer took his time to answer, wondering if it would take more energy to answer or ignore the armadillo and his cat friend. Finally, he answered in his lowest and most exhausted voice, "Nope. Nothing. Nothing. Nothing..." he softly repeated to himself as he drifted back to sleep.

"This is a waste of time," Henry said growing frustrated, "I am going to just stay out here on the porch all night and see for myself what is going on."

"No, Mr. Baker will come looking for you. You have to go back inside just like Otto said, and I will stay out on the porch and keep a lookout. Don't worry Henry, if I know Otto, he has a plan that will solve this mystery and allow you to live happily here at the Baker's," Arnold said proudly and confidently.

"Well, I suppose. I appreciate all your help," Henry said,

then added, "How long have you known Otto anyway?

"Almost a few days!" Arnold said excitedly, but Henry's face drooped in disappointment and fear.

The two wandered around the rest of the backyard over the course of the day. They strolled around the old wheelbarrow that was parked next to the shed. They found some recently disturbed branches and leaves, as well as a few rusted old tools and an old tire half buried in mud and old leaves, but nothing more. The fence was in good shape, but it was a simple split rail fence, which allowed for almost any animal to come and go. By suppertime, Henry headed back into the Baker's house and Arnold made his way toward the Baker's woodpile and made a feast out of some delicious grubs. As the sun went down, Arnold took up his spot just outside the Baker's back porch as Mr. Baker relaxed there, sitting down with his newspaper and a freshly lit pipe. Arnold could smell the pipe smoke, and it was a very pleasing, almost soothing aroma. Arnold drifted slowly off to sleep.

It wasn't long after dark when Arnold was stirred awake by a sudden cry out from the middle of Mr. Baker's large backyard. The yard was very dark, surround on the edges by tall pine and oak trees. The moon was out in full, but the tree branches and leaves served to block much of the light making the deepest part of the Baker's yard very dark. Arnold grabbed his glasses and flashlight, and shined it out into the yard. He could not see much of anything. He switched off his torch, but kept looking. After a moment, he saw another torch flashing at him from the deep dark part of the yard. He waited, and soon it flashed

Henry

again, very quickly, almost like a signal light on a ship.

Arnold was scared to venture out into the yard, but a signal like this could not be ignored. "What if it was a trap?" he asked himself. "I'm all alone. What if it is the hound?" Just then, Arnold heard a high-pitched moan coming from the other end of the Baker's house, close to where Boomer slept. It was long and frightening, but not nearly as loud as the shrieking of the night before. Arnold turned back toward the dark yard where he saw the light flash two more times quickly. He then decided to make a brave run toward that flashing light. He took a deep breath, and in a leap of faith ran out into the yard, straight into the dark unknown.

He slowed down as he approached the edge of the

yard where the trees were surrounded by large shrubs and bushes. He gazed around into the hedgerow which divided the Baker's yard from their neighbor's. Arnold couldn't see a thing in the faint light of the moon. Only patches of moon light managed to break through – it was the perfect hiding place.

"Psst," a voice called out.

Arnold just froze, scared to death of what might be near.

"Psst!"

He heard again, this time with some more urgency. Then suddenly, Arnold felt a strong force wrap around his neck and pull him backward. At the same time, his mouth was covered so that he couldn't scream for help. He was dragged quickly into a small nest; built on the ground under a large leafy bush. Fearing for his life, Arnold began to wiggle and struggle frantically.

"Shhh! Arnold," a voice said in a loud whisper, "It's me!"

Arnold wasn't sure what to make of it yet. He was still quite frightened. But he calmed down enough for the unknown figure to release his hold over Arnold's mouth.

"Who are you?" Arnold asked, his voice still quivering.

"It's me, my dear Arnold. Only me."

Arnold slowly turned around to look, and as he did he saw that it was Otto, standing majestically before him. A quick smile dashed across Otto's face, as if he was proud to see his plan coming together so wonderfully. Just as fast as it appeared, the smile left, and his face turned back to business. Arnold was so happy and relieved to see his friend.

"What are you doing?" Arnold asked.

"I've been watching you all day long Arnold, and I must say you wasted so much time and energy, yet accomplished very little."

Arnold was very disappointed at his friend's criticism, for he thought he had spent the day gathering valuable clues and interviewing a potential witness. Otto continued, "But you managed to accomplish the most important task of all."

"What was that?" Arnold asked.

"You kept our new friend Henry busy and out of the way. I have done my own bit of investigating today, and I think we shall soon see the fruits of my labor and solve this mystery once and for all. But you must stay close to me Arnold, and do exactly as I say."

Arnold agreed, and was now full of suspense and excitement. Otto instructed Arnold to stay close no matter what happened. Both were poised to move into action at a moment's notice, but what kind of action Arnold had no idea. Then the loud shrieking noise erupted from about half way across the darkened yard, between Otto and Arnold and the
Baker house. It was fantastically loud, much louder and more desperate than the cries from the night before.

Arnold's heart began to pound so hard that he thought it might explode out of his chest! But Otto kept whispering softly, "Not yet. Not yet."

After what seemed like eternity, something else stole their attention and brought the shrieking to an end. It was a low sound that came from the far side of the Baker house. It began as a moan and then grew into a more terrifying growl. Otto crouched down as if he was prepared to pounce on his prey during a hunt!

Then in a flash, out of the left side of the yard came a giant figure lunging into the center of the yard at great speed! To Arnold, it appeared to be a giant ghost hound glowing clearly through the dark as moonlight cascaded all around him. He tore from the side of the house like lightening streaking through the sky, and his growling became intense mixed with evil sounding barks and howls! He appeared to be running both at top speed and in slow motion at the same time, his muscles flexing and his body burning streaks of lights across the long dark yard.

"Now!" Otto yelled and took off in the direction of the giant hound. Arnold was too stunned to run along with him and remained with his feet planted firmly to the ground, his mouth wide open in stunned silence. But then he remembered Otto's instructions to remain by him no matter what, and fearing that he might be in even more danger by staying where he was, he finally took to his heels and ran off after his friend.

Before he could reach the center, he saw and heard a swirl of violent activity where the ghost hound apparently ran into Otto. Arnold continued to run to help, fearing the hound was tearing his friend to pieces as the screams of terror and pain came from seemingly all directions. And then, just before Arnold reached the site of all the action, it suddenly all stopped and was quiet.

"There! That is the source of your mysterious shrieking!" announced Otto. He apparently survived the struggle with only a minor cut to his head, just above his left eye. Standing to his right was the ghost hound, glowing bright like some glow-in-the-dark toy. And between them, lay a very large stray cat – the hound holding him down to the ground with his foot. It was clear that the stray cat was literally scared to death! The hound lifted up his foot, and the cat tore off as fast as he could into the woods.

"I don't understand!" Arnold cried. "What happened? Who is that?"

Just then, Henry arrived on the scene looking worried. "I just heard all the commotion, and then I heard you Arnold, and Otto, what has happened?" Henry asked.

"I shall explain everything," Otto began. "But first, I must thank my friend here. Well done, Boomer! Well done indeed!"

"Thank you." Boomer replied in his more normal mellow tone of voice.

"Boomer?" Arnold questioned. "But how?"

"It was simple." Otto began again. "When you took Henry on your investigation, I followed around and did some investigating on my own. Once I was sure there was nothing else in the yard that could have possibly made such noise last night I concluded that it had to be the stray cat that has been hanging around as of late. He was trying to wreak so much havoc on the Baker's that they would throw Henry out of the house, blaming him for the screams. The stray would then hope to be taken in by the Baker's and living in comfort for the rest of his life. You see Arnold, once you eliminate the impossible, whatever remains, however improbable must be the truth."

Otto continued, "I then approached Boomer and asked him to wait out of sight tonight. I knew the legend of the old hound of the Bakers would do the trick to scare off this pitiful excuse for a cat. Once he knew that the legend was true and the house was guarded by the ghost hound, he'd run far away and never return."

"But Boomer really looked like a ghost. How did you do that?" Henry asked?

"Mr. Baker had a supply of phosphorous powder, for his garden, which glows in the dark. I spilled it and had Boomer roll around in the powder until it covered him. Then I had Boomer sit under the front porch light all evening until he heard the shrieking." Otto explained. "Then he emerged and attacked the stray just as planned."

"But you let him get away!" Arnold added.

"Of course!" Otto exclaimed. "I want him to tell everyone that the legend is true! The hound lives on at the Bakers!" Otto smiled proudly as he pointed toward Boomer who then took a bow as if he was being applauded for a fantastic performance.

"So you mean, I'm free to live here and there is nothing else to fear? No real hound or anything?" Henry said, with tears forming in his eyes from the pure joy he was feeling.

"Exactly, my friend. You have nothing more to fear than a good nights sleep and happy living the rest of your days with excellent owners, and a friend of a hound dog." With these words, all the friends cheered and laughed!

"What about your promise to me?" Boomer asked Otto.

"Oh yes, of course. There is one little thing you must do

Henry." Otto said.

"Anything! I owe you so much Otto, anything at all!" Henry said.

"I promised Boomer here that you would furnish him with an ample supply of bacon whenever Mrs. Baker cooks it, which I believe is every Sunday morning for breakfast.

"It's a deal, of course!" Henry replied with a laugh and a smile. He and Boomer shook hands, and then departed back home to get a good night sleep. "Thank you both again!" Henry said as they walked away.

"My pleasure! Arnold said. Any time we can be of help, we'll be here!" Arnold was now very confident and proud of himself and his friend Otto. "Wait until Ellen and Andy hear about this!" Arnold exclaimed.

"Oh yes, well, you're the writer, my dear Arnold. You are much better at turning such a beautiful exercise of logic into a grand piece of fiction with all your embellishments and exaggerations!" said Otto.

"I do tell a good story, don't I?" Arnold asked.

"Yes, you do. And I couldn't have accomplished this without you. You did quite well, Arnold." Otto replied.

"Thank you!" said Arnold, gratified by the compliment.

Just then, as the two headed for home, Arnold heard a soft voice coming from the corner of the yard near the woodpile. They ran over to investigate.

"Arnold? Is that you?" a girl's voice softly asked.

"Yes, who's there?" Arnold replied.

"It's me Arnold. It's Irene!"

Overjoyed at seeing his friend again, Arnold was quick to embrace her and he began to tell her about all his adventures since he began living with Ellen and Andy. After a few days spent together, it quickly became clear to Arnold that his feelings for Irene were growing deeper.

"Arnold, are you falling in love?" Ellen asked with a big smile on her face.

"Me? In love with Irene? No, I don't think so." Arnold quickly denied. He had been in the habit of denying his feelings for Irene since before he stumbled under the garden wall and into Ellen and Andy's yard. But in the back of his mind, he knew that Irene had always been, for him, "the woman" and that she was indeed the love of his life.

Chapter 5

A Mid-summer Night
Armadillo's Dream

Part I – A Rose by Any Other Name

Look, Arnold! A robin!" Andy shouted from across the backyard. It wasn't uncommon to see robins around the yard, but they usually flew north during the summer and so this was a pretty rare sight. Arnold caught a glimpse of his red tummy before he flew off high into a nearby tree. Andy ran over to Arnold. "Did you see it? Did you, Arnold?"

"Yes! I saw it. What's so amazing about that bird anyway?" Arnold asked.

"Robins are magical, Arnold. Some say that they bring the springtime and with it all the flowers and the warm sunshine! But I heard that they also cast spells to make anything grow." Andy continued.

"Wow!" gasped Arnold. "That is one amazing bird. A miracle, magical bird!"

"Like a fairy." Ellen chimed in as she walked over to get Andy. "Daddy's calling us, we're going to the planetarium today with some friends. We'll be back for supper Arnold."

"Bye!" Arnold shouted. But he didn't think going somewhere to watch plants sounded like much fun. *Humans are somewhat strange creatures*, he thought.

The days are long and warm in the summertime. Arnold had been spending the long days catching up with Irene, his long lost armadillo friend. It wasn't long before Ellen and Andy had fashioned another pair of armadillo glasses for her, and she was able to speak with everyone just like Arnold. She quickly learned new words and discovered new ways of expressing herself like she had never known before. She took to reading and found great joy in acting out scenes from plays Ellen and Andy shared with her, Arnold, Otto, and Henry.

Otto in particular referred to her as the most fascinating woman he had ever encountered. "She seems very wise," he declared. "For an armadillo." She explained how she had shown up a few weeks earlier because she was running away from home. There was a bigheaded, rich armadillo named Cornelius who wanted her to marry him, but she had refused. He was strong and an up and coming leader of their armadillo pack who wouldn't leave her alone. He even pressured her father who then promised she would marry him. But Irene was too strong willed, and because she didn't love him, she ran away. She remembered the woodpile from months ago, and that Arnold had been lost there. She knew he would still be her friend if she found him. And as luck would have it, she did just that.

But catching up with Irene meant more to Arnold than anyone else. He had always been in love with Irene, and now fate had brought them together. He was thrilled at the idea that she might be in love with him and that it was destiny for them to meet again. The sad part was that Irene didn't seem to notice or return his feelings. Finally, as Ellen and Andy headed inside for the night, Irene asked Arnold if he'd walk her home, across the yard. He was delighted, and as they walked in the fading sunlight, she told him a secret.

"I've missed you so much Arnold. We always had such fun playing together, bumping into things, and laughing,"

Irene started.

"I remember laughing with you too. I never laughed so hard as that time when we tricked Willie into believing you had laid an egg in the duck's nest!" Arnold began to laugh as he spoke, Irene joined in with his laughter.

"We had such fun when we were young. I wish it could be spring time forever." Irene said as she stopped and looked straight into the sky, her eyes open as wide as they could as if she was seeing the world around her for the very first time. "I had no idea that stars even existed!" she said. Thanks to her new glasses, she saw them for the very first time.

"I know. There's so much more to life then what we armadillos can see" Arnold said proud of himself for sounding so intelligent and deep.

"Yes, there is much more to life than running around, eating worms and grubs, and doing what everyone else expects you to do. I don't want to live by someone else's idea of happiness. I want to be happy, and I want to be able to love the armadillo I want to love!" Irene said defiantly. Her speech almost took Arnold's breath away, for he felt in his heart that she was talking about him.

"I know just how you feel," he said, gazing into her eyes as her eyes gazed at the stars.

"I'm in love Arnold" Irene continued, still focused on the sky above. "I'm in love and I can't even show it, how terrible and meaningless is that?"

"I think you can show it, Irene" Arnold said, hoping she would turn to him and tell him that she loved him. He continued with an idea that he thought might sway her to

70

open up and tell him she loved him. "How about tomorrow, I take you for a walk in the enchanted garden! I will show you beautiful things like you've never seen before!"

"That sounds nice, Arnold. Thank you. You're so sweet and kind," Irene said. Then she continued, "I wish I could share such an experience with Demetri."

With the sound of the name "Demetri" Arnold's heart sank. He was crushed that she was so taken with someone else. He just lowered his head, and began walking back home alone, leaving Irene gazing wishfully at the stars.

Arnold was too upset to sleep. He laid wide-awake most of the night thinking about what he could do to change her mind. But nothing came to him. Then, just before dawn, the Robin suddenly appeared, landing on the railing of the fort. Arnold quickly put his glasses on and whispered, "You! Mr. Robin could you help me?"

"Of course I will my friend." Robin said as he looked down upon Arnold who was still a bit drowsy from a lack of sleep. "What can I do for you?"

"I want Irene, my armadillo friend, to love me. But she's in love with someone else named Demetri. If you could just make her see that I am the love of her life, I would be forever in your debt." Arnold pleaded.

"Say no more my little armored friend!" Robin proclaimed. "But you will owe me nothing, as I carry no debt and earn no reward for my work!"

"Wow, you are amazing! You must have single-handedly brought about the spring!" Arnold began to lavish his praise upon his new robin friend.

"Well, actually, no." Robin slowly responded. "I was just born this past spring, and I sort of got lost when the others flew north for the summer. So, I'm kind of just waiting around here until they get back." He explained. "I've really never tried this kind of thing before. But I do miss having friends and I'm sure I can make something good happen," Robin concluded.

Robin

"Anything you can do will be a great help," Arnold said, for he had nothing to lose.

"Interesting glasses." Robin stated, looking at Arnold intensely. "Does your friend Irene have a pair as well?"

"Yes, she does," answered Arnold.

"Good!" Robin said, "I have a plan!" and he flew off into the woods. Several minutes later he returned with a small pouch and gave Arnold the following instructions. "All you have to do is wipe this rose color potion onto her glasses when she is asleep. Then in the morning when she wakes and puts them on, she will fall madly in love with the first person she sees!"

"Or Armadillo?" Arnold asked just to be sure.

"Or Armadillo," Robin confirmed.

Arnold was so excited he couldn't fall asleep even for a few minutes before the day began. He began to think about how he'd get Irene to fall asleep so he could wipe the rose color potion onto her glasses. Then, it occurred to him that a nice long walk through an enchanted garden would do the trick!

She'd marvel at all the flowers and colors, but then grow tired in the heat of the day and want to settle down for a short nap. Once asleep, he'd wipe the rose color potion onto her glasses, and when she woke, she would see him as never before and be madly in love with him! What could possibly go wrong?

As soon as the sun was up, Arnold excitedly flew down the slide, flying high into the air (at least it felt that way) and landed on all four feet without so much as a stumble. Today was his day, and he made his way over to Irene's burrow.

Irene was still yawning when Arnold came to call on her.

"Irene! Irene! Are you awake?" Arnold called.

"Of course I am!" cried Irene in reply, "Who could sleep with your calling my name like that?" Irene said with a giggle.

"I am so excited, Irene! I want to take you to the enchanted garden and show you something wonderful!" Arnold proclaimed.

"It sounds wonderful, that's for sure. You're so happy this morning! That's good to see." Irene said as she popped out of the hole that led into her burrow by the large flowerpot. "Let's go!"

Both wearing their glasses, the two went off to the opposite end of the yard, and entered the Baker's backyard through the crack in the fence, which was now used quite often. Boomer was lying there, still sleeping soundly. As the couple passed by Arnold let out a cheerful "Hello, Boomer!" It is not clear whether it was the loudness or cheerfulness of Arnold's voice that annoyed Boomer more. But he opened his eyes, and even lifted an eyebrow in order to investigate what was going on, before taking a deep breath and drifting quickly back to sleep. The two armadillos strolled by, sniffing the grass in search of breakfast along the way.

They stopped by the Baker's woodpile to eat some grubs and bugs. Irene dug just deep enough to come up with a fat juicy worm, which she showed off, to Arnold. Arnold was more in love than ever before at the site of

Irene holding a fat, juicy worm in her hand and watching her sip it into her mouth like a long strand of spaghetti.

Once they finished breakfast, they headed toward the far back of the yard and toward the front of Mrs. Widmer's house where the gate was located. Mrs. Widmer had kept her yard very secure ever since Arnold had tangled with her windmill and lost, so Irene had never been there before. Arnold remembered the trick about opening the gate however, which was to simply push on it. But Arnold decided to put on a show of strength for Irene and so he rubbed the side of the gate, then pushed his read-end up against the front, and then pretended to push with all his might! But the gate didn't budge as he expected and he found himself actually pushing, turning around and pushing more, and then turning back around to use his hind legs and read-end again for a maximum push! But still, nothing happened.

Then Irene noticed that there was a gap between the wood plank on which Arnold was pushing, and the one next to it. She gently pushed on the plank next to where Arnold had been struggling, and the gate gently and smoothly swung open. Arnold immediately stopped. He realized he had been pushing up against the post, which stood right next to the gate and not on the gate itself. Irene looked at him, smiled bashfully, and then giggled. Arnold laughed along with her, but inside he was completely dejected.

Nevertheless, the two made their way into Mrs. Widmer's backyard and into what Arnold had called, the enchanted garden. Irene's eyes opened wide amidst the vast array of colors, shapes, and smells of the garden before her. Sunflowers towered over them to their right, and daisy's filled a patch on their left. The pathway was made of freshly laid cedar chips which smelled like a feast, and the larger trees and bushes which lined the path seemed to be taking them truly into a dream world. They spent an hour or so roaming around the rose garden, then came across some tulips. Every so often they would spy a ceramic frog, one playing the violin, and the sound of trickling water seemed to surround them. The first fountain had three bowls, the smallest at the top, which overflowed into a slightly larger bowl, and that one into the large bottom bowl that was near the ground. They took a drink from it as the water cascaded down around them like a magnificent waterfall.

More than anything, Irene realized that with her glasses she could actually see the world around her now in such vivid and wonderful ways; it was as if someone had opened a door into a whole new world. She had been walking around in the same space as before but never able to notice all the beauty and wonder it contained. Life itself seemed new and fresh again. It was amazing to think that the flowers, the clouds in the sky, and creatures of all kinds, had been there all along but only now did she realize them and appreciate their unique beauty – something she noticed that every single living thing possessed, a unique inner beauty. How blind she had been before. It was all the same, yet all new and unbelievable.

There was so much more to life than what she realized before – she began to wonder if there was something still greater beyond what even now she could see. Perhaps there was still more she could not? These thoughts mesmerized her throughout their walk. Could this all be just a dream?

They reached a small grassy glade in the center of the garden, which seemed a perfect spot to rest.

"I don't know about you Irene, but I could sure use a nice
relaxing nap!" Arnold said, hoping she'd agree and that once she fell asleep he would paint Robin's potion onto her glasses.

Irene took a long, deep breath and smiled. "Yes, I am overwhelmed Arnold. Just look at all these incredible things! It is all so incredible, so bright, so alive! I think I do need a nap just to soak it all in!" As she finished speaking, she gave a long yawn followed by a very unexpected and loud burp.

"Huh? Oh, my. Excuse me," Irene said embarrassed. But Arnold couldn't help but laugh, and when Irene joined in he just loved her all the more!

The two took off their glasses and settled down for a nap. Arnold managed to stay awake until he was sure Irene was sleeping, and then he moved over to her glasses and opened Robin's pouch of rose-colored potion. Once he opened the pouch he poured it all over her glasses. He wiped them carefully to make sure it covered every part of the lenses, and then with his mission now complete. Since he had not slept much the night before, Arnold fell asleep almost as soon as his head hit his soft grassy pillow. He was finally able to relax assured that soon Irene would wake up and fall in love with him forever.

Part II – Where for art thou, Arnold?

A sharp and insistent bark startled Arnold and Irene from their slumber. The high-pitched bark was followed by a puny growl and then another bark. Arnold and Irene stood at attention, their defensive instincts taking over. Instantly they both rushed to pick up their glasses and turn to run away.

But just before each of them managed to get their glasses on, they ran straight into each other, bumping their heads, and sending both of them back onto their rear-ends dazed and confused.

The barking was coming from Penni, Mrs. Widmer's little Yorkie dog who was actually barking more out of fear than anything else. But her barking calls immediately attracted Mrs. Widmer, who armed herself with a broom and headed in their direction.

As soon as Arnold and Irene recovered from their stunning bump into each other, they both took off in opposite directions. Irene escaped under a bush near the fence, which led into an unknown neighbor's backyard. She began digging frantically until she squeezed through with all her might and left Mrs. Widmer's yard. Arnold on the other hand, managed to plow straight into Mrs. Widmer's fence.

"Ouch! I didn't need that!" Arnold cried as he once again found himself on his backside. But then he instantly remembered why he couldn't see where he was going. He needed his glasses! With them, he would be able to easily figure out where he was and how best to escape. He turned around and quickly scrambled to find his glasses, which were only a few feet away.

"Who's there?" Mrs. Widmer's powerful voice bellowed through the garden as she was getting closer and closer. Arnold continued to search for his glasses, finding them just in time. He hastily placed them on his head and began to look around. But just as soon as he noticed that he could see clearly again, he also realized that the world also looked slightly rose colored. Before he could correct his mistake, Mrs. Widmer appeared over him holding her broom high above her head ready to strike! Arnold turned toward her, and was suddenly still, calm, and happy. A smile grew upon his face as he gazed up at Mrs. Widmer. Arnold was in love!

As Mrs. Widmer continued to threaten and shake the broom over her head trying to scare Arnold away, Arnold instead began to slowly walk toward her. He was in a complete trance! He was madly in love with Mrs. Widmer and he wanted to go over and talk to her. Usually armadillos run away, so Mrs. Widmer grew frightened and began to walk backward as this showdown continued. As Arnold moved out from the edge of the garden and onto the main part of the backyard, Penni was overwhelmed by her fear and took off for the safety of the house.

"Go away!" shouted Mrs. Widmer. "Go away" she said again, this time in a lower more serious tone. She looked at him with piercing eyes, trying to contain her own fright.

But to Arnold, her message was confusing. He was in love with her, why should she want him to go away? So he stood up onto his hind legs and said as clear as day, "Oh Mrs. Widmer, how I love thee!"

Arnold reached out his hands as if to embrace her, but Mrs. Widmer threw the broom straight up into the air and ran frantically back toward her house yelling, "It talked! It talked! The armadillo talked! Ahhhh!"

"Oh, my love! Don't play hard to get," Arnold said in a low calm voice, as if Mrs. Widmer could hear him over her own screams. She ran inside and slammed the door. The only other sound left was the clicking noise of the deadbolt securely locking it behind her.

Arnold casually followed her to the door. Along the way he noticed how much more beautiful the world seemed to be with these rose colored glasses! The flowers were brighter and smelled even more lovely, and even the garden gnomes seemed to be smiling with joy because he was in love. Arnold stopped at the back door which was painted in a soft white color with green stems of vines rising up along its sides, with little purple flowers poking out every so often.

"To take such great care of a back door reveals a truly remarkable owner!" Arnold reveled in his thoughts of Mrs. Widmer. Then she appeared from the window of the door high above Arnold and looked out not noticing Arnold straight below. Arnold stood up suddenly and said, "But, soft! What light through yonder window breaks? It is the east, and Mrs. Widmer is the sun!"

The fact that she had a talking armadillo on her back porch so frightened Mrs. Widmer that his words fell on deaf ears. She screamed again, and ran upstairs and called the police. But Arnold continued, "It is my lady, Oh, it is my love! Oh, that she knew she were!"

By now others around the yard had begun to take notice, thanks to Mrs. Widmer's screams. Otto had seen the commotion from atop his fort tower and quickly wondered over to investigate. He picked up Henry from next door and even managed to rouse Boomer to join him, and they all soon arrived at Mrs. Widmer's gate and were watching Arnold standing now below her bedroom window that was off to the left of her porch. Other animals and a neighbor boy who lived next door to Mrs. Widmer also peeked over the fence and were staring in amazement! Arnold seemed as if he was under a spell and he continued to call to her.

"My name? My name?" he called to her loudly so that she might hear through the window. "Why my name is Arnold, love! And Widmer is such a sweet name that I shall take it as my own and be called, Arnold Widmer! And yet an armadillo by any other name would not smell as sweet!"

"More like dead worms or trash!" Otto said to Henry and Boomer.

"Armadillos sure don't smell good. Not like bacon," Boomer replied in his low tired tone.

"We have to get him out of here before he gets into serious trouble. If the world discovers a talking armadillo, who knows what will happen to him," Henry explained.

"It's those glasses, look! They are rose colored! Everyone knows that things always look better with rose-colored glasses. We have to rescue him before it's too late!" Otto proclaimed.

"Yes, but how are we going to do that?" Henry asked,

who was quick to follow Otto's train of thought.

"I'll talk him in to coming over to this side of the house. Boomer, that's when you'll grab him, and carry him back home. Henry, when Boomer grabs him, you snatch off those glasses and bring them back with us." The partners agreed, and with the plan in place, Otto walked into the backyard as Arnold continued his soliloquy.

"Arnold!" Otto gave an intense whisper to try and get his attention. But Arnold was still talking endlessly to an empty window and paid him no attention.

"Is love a tender thing? No, it is too rough, too rude, too overexcited, and it pricks like a thorn." Arnold said as he became more and more sad that Mrs. Widmer was not responding.

By now sirens could be heard in the distance, and Otto knew he only had seconds to get Arnold out of there before the police would arrive.

"Over here, Arnold!" he called. "She's over here in this window, come quick before this yonder window breaks!" he said trying to fit in to Arnold's dreamy state of mind. "He must be crazy, that woman's mirror must be covered in duct tape to keep it from shattering every morning she looks into it," Otto said to himself.

Arnold headed over toward Otto and just as he turned the corner, Boomer grabbed him by the neck with his huge mouth, and lifted him high into the air. Henry tried hard to grab ahold of his glasses, but as Arnold struggled and wiggled around, Henry looked like he was swinging at a catnip toy! Finally, the glasses flew off back toward Mrs. Widmer's house. Arnold gave out a loud yelp that scared

Boomer, who thought he may have hurt Arnold, and so he let him go.

Arnold tore back toward the house and put the glasses back on.

"Wait, my love! Wait for me! I am breaking the light of yonder window and love is a many splendid thing!" Arnold shouted. It was clear that he was now becoming very confused and disoriented.

Otto jumped upon Arnold's back and held him down for a moment until Boomer was able to recapture him. Henry finally got the glasses off as Boomer quickly began to carry Arnold back through the gate and eventually home.

As they quickly strolled away from the garden and back home, Arnold shouted out toward Mrs. Widmer, "Good night, and good night! Parting is such sweet sorrow, that I shall say good night till it be morrow."

"There won't be a tomorrow for you at all if we don't get you out of here!" Otto said sharply. But before leaving the garden, Henry couldn't help but wonder if the glasses actually made the world appear so wonderful and different. So, he placed them on his head and gazed back toward Mrs. Widmer's house. It seemed to have no effect. Then he heard Otto call for him.

"Henry! Let's go!" cried Otto.

Just as Henry caught sight of Otto through the rose color glasses, he smiled blissfully and said, "Yes of course, my love! I'm on my way!" and he began to prance over toward Otto.

"You fool! Take those off this instant!" Otto scorned as

he flung them off Henry's face. "Now get going! Hurry!" Otto ordered. Henry ran on as instructed. Otto picked up the glasses and brought them with him following the others out through the gate and back to the Baker's just before the police arrived to investigate.

Without his glasses, the spell soon wore off and Arnold grew incredibly tired and fell fast asleep once again. Boomer went home, and Otto left Arnold alone to sleep in his bed. Just then, Robin returned and landed next to him and flew down toward Arnold's rose-colored glasses. Arnold woke for a moment, still very dazed and confused.

"If I have offended, think but this, and all is mended," Robin said to the wary armadillo. "That you have but slumbered here while these visions did appear; and this weak and crazy scene was nothing but a dream."

With that, Robin wiped away the rose color from his glasses, and Arnold fell back to sleep faster than Boomer after being disturbed by a fly landing on his nose.

The next morning, Arnold woke with all his friends gathered around. Otto had told Ellen and Andy about what happened. When they asked Arnold about his day and where Irene had gone, he really couldn't say. He didn't seem to remember much of anything.

"It seemed like a dream," said he. But he noticed that it was no dream that Irene had not returned. "Maybe she is gone forever now, and she will never know that I love her." With this Arnold began to cry. Ellen and Andy took turns holding and comforting him until he began to feel a little better.

From atop a tree across the yard, Robin had been

watching. He had seen everything take place and spoke softly out loud even though no one else was able to hear him, "Be cheerful, my friend. We are all merely actors and are melted into thin air. The world is like a vision. All the towers, gorgeous palaces, and solemn temples, even the entire earth itself, will someday dissolve like a cloud. We are such stuff as dreams are made of, and our little life is rounded with sleep."

Chapter 6

The Tell-Tale Armadillo

When Arnold woke on Halloween morning, he was not a happy armadillo. The dream, which nagged at him in the night, was now alive in his mind throughout the daytime as well. Nearby, overlooking the Fort that Arnold now called his home, a raven stood perched high above in a tree – keeping an eye on him.

"Once upon a midnight dreary, while I pondered, weak and weary, thoughts of the love I'd lost not long before, there came a tapping, of a raven gently rapping, upon my chamber door. He spoke of how he too lost his love, Lenore – quoth the raven, Nevermore." These were the last words Otto had said to him the night before in order to put him into the mood of Halloween. But he didn't have nightmares, only dreams of Irene, which only served to depress him. She hadn't been heard from for months now, and it seemed unlikely that he would ever see her again. The poem Otto had shared didn't do much to cheer him up.

Pumpkins decorated the front porches of all the houses in the neighborhood that Halloween night. All of the kids were soon to be out trick or treating and gathering candy which, for some, would last months! The anticipation for this holiday had been terribly difficult for Arnold to control. He had always loved nice juicy grubs, roaches, beetles, and worms. That slimy, sometimes crunchy goodness always felt so wonderful in his mouth as he chewed them up for a delicious meal. But ever since he met Ellen and Andy, he had also been introduced to various human foods, and Arnold could never get enough of it, especially candy.

So when Ellen had finished explaining the concept of

"trick or treat" to him, his mind became consumed with thoughts of piles and piles of chocolate candies, gumdrops, and sweet lollipops! Surely this would be the most incredible dream come true for him.

"Yes, it's true." Henry, who was visiting that afternoon, reassured Arnold who had asked whether or not he was aware of the candy tradition. "But you're an armadillo, and I am a cat. We don't go and "trick or treat," we just sit around and perhaps pick up a lost candy or two from the sidewalk after everyone else is through."

That didn't sound like much fun. Arnold was crushed by the news that his candy dreams would not be coming true after all. Ellen had not mentioned that he couldn't go with them. But as he thought about it, he realized it was true. No armadillo could go and yell "trick or treat" and receive candy. It just wasn't fair!

Arnold took off down the slide and into the backyard. He decided he would go for a walk to calm down. If he was lucky, maybe he'd find and extra plump cockroach, which would at least feel crunchy, like a candy bar in his mouth. After about an hour, he returned to the tower fort, and nervously sat down next to his bed. Henry looked at him curiously.

"Where have you been?" Henry asked.

"Nowhere," Arnold answered, his voice trembling along with the rest of his body. "Why? Did someone come looking for me?" he asked.

"No. You just seem a little nervous." Henry said.

"Can you keep a secret, Henry?" Arnold asked.

"Of course!" Henry said with excitement.

"I mean, a real secret. Something you cannot share with anyone!" Arnold insisted.

"Yes, yes! I promise" said Henry.

So Arnold began, "True! – Nervous – very, very nervous. But I am not crazy. No! Why would you say I am crazy? If anything, I am more focused and sure of myself than ever before! You see! Yes, I am calm now. Very calm indeed that I can tell you the whole story."

"I don't know how the idea came to me, but it just did," Arnold continued, "it just popped into my head like a piece of toast popping out of the toaster. I always liked Mrs. Dykwell, she always seemed to like it when I visited to drink from her little bird bath."

"Who is Mrs. Dykwell?" Henry asked.

"She's the widow who lives alone next door to Ellen and Andy, on the opposite side from the Bakers," Arnold answered.

"Oh, well, I hope you have a nice Halloween, Arnold. I have to go home and eat my supper, bye!" Henry said as he promptly climbed down the back way out of the Fort which was attached to the swing set. But Arnold was too lost in thought to have noticed, and continued to tell his story to no one in particular.

Arnold continued, "She never bothered me in the least, Mrs. Dykwell, but one of her eyes was cloudy and bluish in color. I think it must have been that eye which made my blood run cold. And when I saw that she had left a basket full of candy out on her front porch with a sign that said, "Please take one," I knew that I could do it! The better part of me knew I shouldn't, for she was always kind to me. But then I remembered her cloudy blue eye, an evil eye if I ever saw one, and so I knew I could do it! I knew I would take all her candy and keep it for myself!" Arnold said with great excitement, and a proud but sinister smile and gaze.

"Now you might think I'm crazy, but it isn't me, it is the sweet goodness of that human food known as candy! Because if I was crazy, I wouldn't have been so careful. I would have just stormed over to Mrs. Dykwell's house and leapt into the basket full of candy and eaten it all right there! But no. I moved in very slowly, spying on the activities around me and carefully measuring their movements. The squirrel across the yard, the old man walking his dog down the street, and even the raccoon hiding out in the bushes just across the street thinking no one knew he was there. But I knew! I knew the wind speed, the humidity, and the approximately weight of all that chocolaty flavor being stored in the basket above my head.

"It was still daylight, so I strolled confidently onto her front porch as if I were conducting business elsewhere. I walked up there and behind the little table on which the basket was resting. It was all just perfectly normal. No one looking on would have suspected a thing! I made myself look like a busy armadillo, running back and forth looking for grubs. Yes, back and forth I went in a hearty manner, occasionally asking a blue bird how things were going and if all was well in her world. She knew nothing!"

"As I turned the corner on the opposite side of the house, I quickly darted back and took up my position tightly snug against the red brick wall. Then, slowly, ever so slowly so as not to be noticed by even a mosquito, I moved my head around until I could just barely make out the delectable candy delights only a few feet away. I'd stare at it as if I could already taste it. But nothing made me act. There was nothing as of yet to stir my conscious. So I went on normally once again, back toward the other side of the house as if busy running errands and paying the table, basket, and candy no mind – as if they didn't even exist at all.

"On the eighth run back toward the opposite side of the house, I was even more cautious. I moved even more carefully and slowly around the corner to watch the candy. To think that that raccoon across the street still had no idea of my plans or thoughts. To think that blue bird believed everything around her to be perfectly normal. But no, I knew that soon it would all come falling down and I'd make off with all that candy treasure!"

"Just then I heard a voice – 'Who's there?' it cried from just below the porch. It was a tiny little chipmunk that had peeked out from a small hole under the concrete step leading to the porch. He must have heard the rustling of some leaves as I walked across just before. I remained still and quiet, peering from behind the wall only a couple of feet away. His little nose sniffed the air around him, but I was careful mind you, oh so careful, to take up a position downwind of his little nasal sensor. He could not possible detect me!

"Did I draw back? But no! I knew he couldn't see me, and I knew he couldn't hear or smell me, so I kept still for what must have been an hour long! But he didn't return to his hole, he kept sniffing and wondering around, but never more than a couple of steps outside his hole. He knew there was danger near, he could feel it. And then, my toe slipped and struck a small twig, which snapped. The chipmunk suddenly froze like an ancient statue. He was now certain of something sinister, but what it was he could not possible know. It seemed that the world around us, so alive with chirps of birds and noises of all kinds, suddenly grew completely silent and still – like a watch enveloped in cotton. It was the sound of a beating heart, and it was the sound of candy!"

"The sound of the heart continued to grow louder and louder, as it pulsed with anticipation at this once in a lifetime opportunity to have all the chocolate candy goodness ever imagined! But still, I kept so steady and still. Yet, the heart grew more powerful and rapid. Finally, after several minutes, that chipmunk's time had come! With all my might I leaped far off onto the top of that chipmunk so fast that he never saw me coming! I screamed once, and only once, so loudly that the trees shook in fright! And that little chipmunk raced so fast and so hard to be away from me that he missed his hole and ran straight into the cement slap, knocking him out cold. He would trouble me no more.

"If you still think I'm crazy, you won't once I tell you about how carefully I retrieved all that candy! Once the coast was clear and the chipmunk gone, I proceeded to climb the stair onto the front porch where a large potted plant was positioned next to the small table, which held the basket of candy. I pushed carefully the pot closer to the basket, and then bent the plant over as if it were blowing in the wind. Yes, nature itself would be blamed for knocking over the basket of candy, Mrs. Dykwell having left it too close to the plant on her porch. Within a few moments, I was successful in using the plant to spill the candy onto the porch. It was a steam of glittering delight as the candy wrappers glistened in the slowly dimming light of the evening."

"I used an old towel from the garage to wrap up my treasure and to drag it back over to my home in our backyard. The towel not only helped me carry all the candies, but also muffled the sound and so drew no attention from anyone. Yes, I was so careful to return here without being detected, and to hide the candy just below this very floor! Down under this very Fort. I removed one of the stone pavers and found a soft spot in the ground. I dug a small passage under the side planks of the wooden swing set. I left the candies still wrapped and inside the towel, and replaced the dirt and the paver. No one would ever know!"

It was then that Arnold finally turned around and noticed that Henry was not there.

"Henry? Henry!" Arnold called out for his friend. Once he realized what he had said, he was glad Henry had not been there to listen. He could finally rest easy now knowing that his candy was safe below and that no one else would ever find out what happened. "Someone else would have taken all her candy if I had not," Arnold figured, "And why should I be left out of Halloween tricks or treats? If I were a human, I would be able to go out and collect all the candy I want, even more than Mrs. Dykwell had left out."

Arnold continued to reassure himself, and just as he was feeling better, he noticed a couple of people approaching. One was dressed all in black, with a pointed hat and carrying a withered old broom. The other was also cloaked completely in black, with only two red eyes glowing in the dusk. Then there was a knock at the fort entrance.

"Boo!" shouted the two strangers as they leapt up right in front of Arnold just as he approached the entrance. Arnold let out a frantic scream and must have jumped two feet straight up into the air, knocking down his dinner plates and bowls, which he stored in a small cupboard just above his supper table.

"Did we scare you Arnold?" asked one of the strangers. "Don't worry, it's only us!" The voice was Andy's as he and Ellen removed their masks to show Arnold their friendly faces.

"Yes! Yes, you did! Oh boy, I was so scared." Arnold said as he hobbled back across the little room to sit down next to his bed. He looked very tired.

"Don't be scared, Arnold, it's only us. We're sorry for frightening you," Ellen tried to console him.

"We just wanted to come by and show you our costumes, Arnold," Andy continued, "what do you think? Do I look like a real phantom?"

"A what? A phantom?" Arnold answered. "I don't know. I'm not sure what a phantom is or what one looks like."

"How about me?" Ellen asked, "Do I look like a witch?"

"Yes, I suppose you do," Arnold said, adding, "but

you're not really a witch because you weigh more than a duck!" he said laughing.

"That's right! You remember how to tell if someone is a real witch or not, don't you!" Ellen smiled proudly recalling some silly stories she had once told him.

"So when do you go trick or treating?" Arnold asked, becoming more nervous. He was thinking about the candy hidden below.

"I don't know," Andy replied. "I want it really dark so my eyes will glow!"

"Well," Arnold continued, adjusting his glasses nervously, "You might want to get out there before someone takes all the candy. I mean, before others take it. I mean, before people run out of it. No?" Arnold asked, rambling from thought to thought. But Ellen and Andy didn't seem to notice his strange behavior, and instead made themselves more at home and relaxed.

But just as he too was beginning to relax, he heard what sounded like a ringing in his ears. It was like static on the radio. It was faint at first, but then it grew as if someone were trying to tune in a new station but there were none to be found.

"I wonder what will become of all the pumpkins after Halloween," Arnold joined in the conversation, pleasantly, in order to shift his mind away from the noise. But the noise kept going, so he realized that it must not be something he was imagining, it was something coming from outside the room.

Arnold got up and paced the floor as Ellen and Andy continued to chat pleasantly to each other. The noise was becoming more distinct now, something much more clear. It was the collective sound of candy wrappers being stirred in a basket, or the sound they make when someone is struggling to open one.

Oh, God! What could I do? Thought Arnold as the sound increased.

"What do you think Arnold, doesn't it sound like fun?" Ellen asked him.

But he hadn't been paying attention and so he simply smiled pleasantly and answered, "Yes, of course, it does sound like fun!"

But even as he spoke the noise grew louder – louder – louder! But still they chatted as if nothing could be heard. But surely they could hear it! It was very clear now, as if giant candy wrappers were dancing in a giant chorus line around the fort and throughout the entire backyard!

They must suspect that something has happened, Arnold thought. *They must know about Mrs. Dykwell, the candy, oh even that blasted chipmunk!* Arnold ranged inside his head! *They are now just making fun of me,* thought he. *Why do they smile at me like that as if they can't hear that noise?*

The crinkling and curling of foil-like candy wrappers now seemed to drown out Ellen and Andy's voices, and yet they seemed not to notice or to care.

Why would they not leave already? Arnold thought. *Why? Why!*

He paced over and over, round and round in a circle over the very floor on which he had buried the candy. He insisted to himself that they knew it. The noise grew even louder, the pacing grew even faster, and his heart was racing until he felt is might explode! Finally, he felt like he must scream or die! The static noise grew louder! Louder! Louder! Louder!

"Villains!" Arnold shrieked. "I cannot take this anymore! I admit the deed! – Tear up the paver and dig into the ground, here! Here, are Mrs. Dykwell's hideous candies!"

Ellen and Andy sat there with their mouths wide open in shock as Arnold revealed his hiding spot and the shiny wrappers of his stolen candy treasure. Ellen lectured Arnold on why it was wrong to take someone else's things.

"That's it!" Arnold declared. "I will never eat another candy as long as I live! I don't want to ever feel that way again. I was scared you wouldn't love me anymore!" Arnold began to sob.

"Oh, Arnold!" Andy said as he reached out and took him into his arms. "We love you no matter what! We all make mistakes."

"Yeah, and we're still trying to teach you" Ellen added. "The important thing now is that you learn from this and know better next time."

"I will do better. I am a good armadillo, I know I am."

"Yes, you're a great armadillo, Arnold!" Andy declared. "And you don't have to give up on candies! We have a surprise for you!"

Just then, Andy pulled a small costume out of his back pack and showed it to Arnold. "It was mine when I was a baby! It's a chipmunk costume, Arnold!"

"A chipmunk?" Arnold said with a little bit of discomfort.

"Yeah, and we're taking you trick or treating!" Ellen announced with excitement.

They returned the candy to Mrs. Dykwell's house and went off to begin trick or treating. Arnold was happy to not be greedy after all, and to play by the rules and be rewarded with candy that he could enjoy with his best friends.

Arnold knew he was the luckiest armadillo in the world to have such great friends. He also realized that he wouldn't have been nearly so lucky if he hadn't made mistakes, because otherwise he would never have known how great it felt to be forgiven and how great it feels to forgive someone else. He also realized that he has a strong conscience, which he'd listen to now more than ever, and that the bond of trust between friends was the most precious gift one could ever be given. It was all a touch of beauty, which survives in dark places.

As they all walked out of the backyard toward the street, the raven, which had been standing high above in the tree next to the swing set, took off into the dark sky. Quoth the raven, "Nevermore!"

Chapter 7

Arnold in Slumberland

Plump, juicy turkey, stuffing, fluffy potatoes with homemade gravy, flaky buttermilk biscuits, tangy fruit salad, sweet cranberry sauce, green and black olives, carrots, celery, baked green bean casserole, sweet potato casserole, and of course, scrumptious pumpkin, and pecan pie! As an armadillo that lusted after human food, even the smallest whiff of bacon would turn his head and start him drooling, this particular holiday was a dream come true! And although he didn't really understand why everyone celebrated by eating such an incredible meal, he quickly understood the meaning of being thankful as Ellen and Andy delivered a warm plate of delicious food to him in the Fort.

"Isn't Thanksgiving great Arnold?" Andy asked as he watched Arnold practically leap up into the air before coming down nose first into the plate of food.

"Yes! Oh, yes, yes, yes!" Arnold managed to shout with his mouth full of turkey and potatoes, bits and pieces of which he spattered across the room and onto Andy and Ellen who laughed as they wiped themselves clean.

"Well, I guess it's okay to go crazy with human food once in a while," said Ellen while laughing at the sight of Arnold smothering his face with cranberry sauce. Arnold couldn't say a word; he just had to keep eating!

"Yeah, but if you eat too much you could get sick. I'd slow down if I were you, Arnold," warned Andy.

Before long, Arnold had finished his humongous plate of food. He plopped down in the middle of the floor, his legs unable to support his weight any longer, and his mouth crusted with pumpkin pie and dripping with a tasty mixture of well-chewed cranberries, olives, turkey, and gravy. He was quite a sight!

"Burrrrrrp!" Arnold belched incredibly loud. Ellen and Andy laughed hard at the sound and the sight of poor Arnold who looked more like a large, fat round stone with little legs sticking almost straight out from each corner of his body. "I don't feel so good!" he cried out.

"Well," Ellen corrected. "You don't feel so well."

"WELL, I don't feel good," Arnold said in an exasperated tone.

"My dad always eats too much at Thanksgiving too," Andy explained. "He usually goes and sits in front of the TV to watch football, unbuttons his pants, and then falls asleep!" Andy and Ellen laughed.

"I'm feeling the same, I guess." Arnold said. "I am very, very tired. I think I will take a nap." He tried to move his legs down to the floor again in order to get up and walk to his bed, but all he could do was wiggle them frantically, as they were unable to touch the ground.

The kids laughed again at the sight before Andy lifted Arnold and carried him to his bed.

"Wow, Arnold!" Andy said as he struggled to lift the fattened armadillo, "You've really packed it in there!"

"Careful Andy, you don't want to squeeze it all back out!" Ellen said with a smirk and a smile.

Arnold fell asleep in no time, and Ellen and Andy went back inside for the evening.

Then all of the sudden, the earth seemed to move below Arnold, a little tremor at first, just enough for him to notice. Then the entire room suddenly swayed to the right. Arnold opened his eyes wide and looked up from his sleep, startled. Then the entire Fort swayed back to the left. The tremor grew into a rocking motion so fantastic that Arnold, now back to his normal size, had to run to the wall and grab a hold of the countertop just to keep his balance. His little pots and pans were tossed from the cupboards, and the swings on the adjoined swing set were rattling and jangling about wildly!

"What's going on?" cried Arnold, but there was no response. As the rocking continued, he noticed that the treetops around him were growing shorter as if the world around him was sinking into the ground. He ran over to the edge of the Fort where he could see the entire yard from atop the slide. But what he saw made him shake with fear. It wasn't that the trees were getting shorter, the entire swing set and Fort was getting taller and taller! In fact, it was growing legs!

Arnold grabbed onto a handle, which attached to the floor at the top of the slide as he was now looking down at the treetops with the four wooden legs of the swing set still growing. They crackled constantly as the legs grew and bent as if hundreds of toothpicks were being snapped at once. Like a newly born horse, these legs were wobbling around and tossing Arnold with them. They hobbled for a moment in the backyard before finally everything settled down. Arnold peaked over the edge down the slide and saw that they were at least three times taller than the houses and trees around them!

"What now?" Arnold cried in panic.

Just then the swing set began to walk! The ride was not smooth for Arnold, but he no longer seemed afraid. They swayed over Mrs. Widmer's fence and stepped over her house as if it were nothing but a small fence. The next step took them into the street in front of Mrs. Widmer's house, then across from there. They continued to step over houses and trees as if they were toys, with the legs of the swing set crackling along the way. Arnold had no idea where they were going, or why, but the ride was proving to be very exciting and he began to smile as the cool air whisked through his wrinkled, scaly skin.

Soon it was clear that they were heading into the woods and out of the neighborhood altogether. They were even taller now, still growing, and the air turned hazy as low clouds swarmed around the Fort. Just as he was wondering how he'd ever get down, he heard a loud sharp call from a peacock.

"What's this?" Arnold asked himself out loud. "A flying peacock?"

Actually, there were two peacocks that flew up through the cloudy haze and hovered just at the bottom of the slide. They were towing a beautiful blue and green colored chariot, which was decorated with shiny stones and crystals. The seat inside was of a dark red, trimmed with a gold color lace. It was fit for a king, but Arnold was certainly not royalty. The peacocks motioned for him to get in, so building up his nerve, he slid down the slide and plopped right into the royal chariot. Immediately, the peacocks took off and Arnold was riding along literally like a bird in the sky – drifting about like a leaf caught in a stream! It was fast and fun, like an incredibly smooth roller coaster. And it was also quiet and peaceful with only the occasional bird call and whistle of the wind blowing by him.

"Where are we going?" Arnold asked of the peacock.

"To see the King!" cried one of the peacocks in return. "He has summoned you, Arnold."

"Me?" Arnold called back. "Why me? What have I done?" But there was no answer. Arnold decided to sit back and enjoy the ride while it lasted. They flew high about the clouds, then down and over some farms and fields. Then they flew almost straight up into the sky, as high as they could manage.

The sky suddenly went completely dark, and Arnold lost all sense of direction, as he suddenly felt very dizzy. The feeling of being spun around and around became almost too much, and just as Arnold began to cry out, everything suddenly stopped.

Arnold opened his eyes to find that he was still in the chariot, but it had landed in what seemed like a grand English garden courtyard. It was neatly decorated with trees and bushes pruned into various animal shapes – one near him, he noticed, was shaped like an armadillo! Arnold smiled with wonder at all the amazing colors and textures of the garden.

"This place makes Mrs. Widmer's garden look like a patch of weeds!" he said.

"Why, thank you," A rough sounding voice replied.

Arnold quickly turned around to see Otto standing next to him. But he was dressed in a light blue suit trimmed with red, and wore a green tie and what looked almost like clown make-up on his face. He had a round top hat on his head which matched his suit, and he was smoking a cigar.

"We have to get going now," the strange looking Otto said, "The carnival will start soon."

"What carnival?" Arnold asked.

"Why, the Carnival of Nations, of course!" answered Otto, who gave a hearty laugh as he put Arnold into a horse drawn carriage while he flipped up to the top and began to drive them down a grand looking avenue.

"The King specifically asked for you, Arnold," Otto said as they entered the gates of a huge palace. The celebratory decorations extended from literally below their feet up into the sky and covered everything in between.

Arnold was in such a trance that he didn't immediately think about what Otto had said, but finally he asked, "What

King? Why ask for me?" By this time hundreds, if not thousands of people had gathered around the palace and were cheering the arrival of Arnold! They were throwing confetti and shouting, "Arnold! Arnold! Arnold!" Arnold was feeling very excited, and yet overwhelmed.

The carriage stopped outside a set of giant golden doors. Otto flipped back down and opened the carriage door. Arnold was hesitant, but finally jumped down onto the red carpet which led up to the giant golden doors. As soon as he was in sight, the crowd roared with applause and cheers as if Arnold was the greatest hero of all time!

"We've all been waiting for you, Arnold!" Otto proclaimed, biting down on his cigar and blowing a sheet of smoke up into the air.

"Me?" Arnold said in amazement. Otto just nodded proudly, and smiled as he gestured toward the golden doors. Arnold moved toward them. As he looked at the doors he noticed that each were engraved with scenes from Arnold's past adventures including riding on the windmill, his trip to Canterbury Park, and the adventure of the Hound of the Baker's. There were also other engravings he didn't recognize, like a puppy in a boat, a frighteningly fierce looking fox, and a giant gnome. And then he saw the engraving of Irene standing in Mrs. Widmer's garden. It was the day he last saw her, and he stopped for a moment as tears began to fill his eyes. Just then the doors swung open and he was ushered in to greet the king.

The long hallway was decorated with gold and silver tables, chairs, candleholders, picture frames, and jewels. It was like walking straight into the most ornate museum you could ever imagine. The colors were hotter and more alive than any he had ever seen before and all of his senses were sharper and more excited than he'd ever experienced. He reached up to wipe his eyes in disbelief, and as he did he realized that all of this was happening and he wasn't even wearing his glasses!

But before he had time to think about it, the king startled him, "No, do not think Arnold! But be happy and welcome to the Carnival of Nations!" he commanded with a deep voice which echoed and resonated throughout the giant hall as if he was speaking into a loud microphone. Everyone erupted in applause and he was led over to meet the princess who was standing off to the side of the king. The princess's servants move aside to reveal her to Arnold. It was Irene!

"Irene!" He yelled! "Is that you?"

"Yes, Arnold! I am here!" as she rushed over to hug him. The crowd cheered as the two loving armadillos held each other for a minute, and then began to walk down the long hallway and out to the back patio of the palace overlooking the grand gardens. The gardens were packed with people and animals like a giant circus! Music and dancing was everywhere!

"The parade is about to begin Arnold, sit here!" Irene showed him to a grand chair next to hers and the King's. There they sat for a long time watching the parade of performers and floats walking by. There was what looked like toy soldiers, horses, unicorns, flying Pegasi, and one amazing thing after another. Then, when the parade finally ended, the King announced to everyone Arnold's official arrival. The crowd cheered and he and Princess Irene took a bow! Fireworks began to shoot up into the sky and lit the garden in beautiful shades of blue, green, gold, purple, red, and every color in between. But then the booms of the fireworks grew very loud and close.

"Those are the cannons!" announced the king who was a bit startled. "That's not supposed to happen! We may be under attack!"

The crowd gasped and began to panic and run for shelter. The King ordered Arnold and Irene into the palace and so Otto led them into a very long hallway, which was lined with statues on both sides.

Arnold and Irene entered the hall alone, and Otto closed the door behind them. It was very quiet as they walked down the hall together. Arnold was focused on Irene like never before and didn't notice the statues they were walking past; they were of various creatures including lions, deer, elephants, and famous soldiers and leaders throughout history.

"I hope this moment never ends, Irene!" he said.

"If you don't think about it, it won't!" she said.

Just then, there was a sound like someone having dropped a glass dish onto the floor, breaking it. Startled, Arnold and Irene looked behind them and saw that one of the statues had broken off from his pedestal, it was a lion statue. Still made of stone, he was able to move and was sniffing and looking around. Then he saw the two armadillos, and bent down as if he were on the hunt!

"Run!" Otto screamed from the other side of the hall, still standing inside the doors. The two wasted no time and took off down the hall. The stone lion quickly leapt into pursuit, chasing them down the hallway with sound of glass shattering with each step. There were no doors on the sides to make an escape, and nothing to hide behind. The little armadillos were simply too slow. Soon the stone lion reached and leapt over them, turned around, and stopped them in their tracks. There they stood, face to face with the huge stone lion. There was no way out.

Part II – Idle Days

They were shaking in fear when the lion calmly said, "Hi, Arnold."

Arnold was a bit stunned by this. He was expecting this lion to crush and then eat him, but instead, his voice sounded very kind and normal. He didn't know what else to do except reply meekly, "Hi."

"Come with me, for I know how to get out of here before it's too late. That army out there is looking for you," the lion said.

"Me? But why?" Arnold asked.

"There's no time to explain. This way." The lion took off toward the side of the hall and tipped over a small statue of a little creature holding what looked like a large tissue and who appeared to be crying. As the statue was tipped, a secret door opened in the wall and the three of them ran out into a courtyard. In the middle of the courtyard was a giant air ship, which looked like a blimp.

"Climb aboard!" called Otto, still dressed in his strange, brightly colored suit. Arnold and Irene quickly scampered aboard and the stone lion wished them well.

"Thank you!" they called down to him as the air ship quickly rose into the night sky. The army cannons fired upon the ship, and fireworks continued to burst all around them. It was a rough and scary ride for a while, but they managed to escape up into the clouds just in time. Looking down on the clouds, they could still hear muffled sounds of fireworks exploding and the glow of softer colors shown through the blanket of clouds below. But it was more peaceful now, and the ship soared with a strong wind at their back.

The airship soon took them across an ocean where the weather began to turn. Lightning flashed through the night sky just below them, and rumbles of thunder seemed to rise up and bump the airship around like a toy. Otto called over to Arnold and the princess that they would need to land soon because the weather was too rough, and to hold on to something as they descended. Arnold and Irene held onto the railing as the ship drifted down into the clouds and into the terrible storm which had been raging below.

"There she is! There's the "Idle Days" shouted Otto at the top of his lungs as he pointed down toward a ship.

"We can make it!" shouted back the captain. "All hands prepare for rescue!"

Arnold and the others took up their positions along the side of the air ship and were ready to throw life preservers and lower a rope ladder to the ship. The ship was rocking around like a tiny leaf caught in a rapids, but the passengers all escaped and the airship took off again and headed for land exhausted from the rough flight. It was clear that they needed to land as soon as possible.

As they approached the shore, the storm let up and they landed smoothly. Arnold and Irene were anxious to escape the rough ride and adventure, as they were both starting to feel a bit queasy. Otto agreed to stay behind and help the passengers while Arnold and Irene began to assess the area for signs of civilization.

The landing spot turned out to be a large beach with a woods beginning just off the water only a few hundred feet away. The forest was very tall, very dark and quiet. All the wind had died down to complete stillness and the sounds of the world seemed to fade into silence. Just then, they heard what sounded like crying coming from the woods.

"Arnold, we need to find out who is crying and help them," Irene said.

"Yes, but we don't know what dangers may be lurking here," Arnold replied. "You stay here, I'll go and find out what is crying. It can't be too far, and I can smell my way back!"

"Be careful Arnold!" Irene said; Arnold loved the fact that she worried about him.

Arnold walked slowly into the forest and soon noticed that the ground below his feet was wet. He sniffed the wet mud with his nose and noticed that it was not fresh rain water, but salty, like tears. In fact, as he moved closer to the crying, the trail became even more soaked with tears. Finally, he reached a small clearing and stumbled upon the creature that turned around, startled and frightened. The two just stared at each other for a moment. The creature was holding a large tissue and dabbing his eyes from time to time, but the tears simply kept falling. He was a long, skinny, rat-like creature with a hairy face with what looked like large moles and corns lined around his very large, deep sad eyes.

"Who are you?" Arnold asked.

"I am a squonk," he answered.

"What is a squonk?" Arnold asked.

"A squonk is I," he answered.

"You are a squonk?" Arnold repeated.

"I am a squonk," the squonk replied.

"Why are you crying?" Arnold asked.

"Because squonks cry," he answered.

"But why do squonks cry?" Arnold insisted.

"Because, that's what squonks do," he sighed.

"Are you sad?" Arnold asked.

"Do you cry when you're sad?" asked the squonk.

"Yes, I cry when I'm sad." Arnold answered.

"Then I'm sad," The squonk answered, wiping his eyes.

"Why are you sad?" Arnold asked.

"Because I'm crying!" the squonk answered.

"But why are you crying?" Arnold asked again.

"Because that's what squonks do," He replied.

"Squonks cry?" Arnold asked, wanting to clarify.

"Squonks cry," the squonk confirmed, sobbing through his tears.

"Because squonks are sad," Arnold continued.

"We're sad if we cry," the squonk said.

"So why not stop crying?" Arnold asked.

"Because squonks cry!" the squonk wailed.

"But why are squonks so sad?" Arnold asked.

114

Squonk

"Because, they are squonks!" He burst into tears.

"And you are a squonk," Arnold said.

"A squonk is I," the squonk answered.

"Why is this so hard?" Arnold questioned himself. But this comment only made the squonk cry harder still. Just then, they heard a twig snap nearby, and the squonk suddenly became very quiet.

"Shhh!" He silenced Arnold. "That's him."

"Who?" Arnold asked.

"The hunter," the squonk whispered.

A moment later a second twig snapped, this time very close to them, and the squonk took off running deeper into the woods. Arnold chased after him, but the squonk was very fast, and he soon fell behind. However, the squonk had left a trail of tears for Arnold to follow, which he did. Soon he could hear the crying again. Arnold stopped for a moment to listen to the crying when he realized that the hunter, whoever he is, would also be able to follow the tear stained trail. The squonk had no chance as long as he kept crying. Arnold finally reached him again and whispered, "You must stop crying or they will find you" he said.

"I cannot stop crying," the squonk whimpered and began to cry harder still.

"Why not? What's wrong?" Arnold asked.

"I am an ugly creature," he said.

"Yes, you certainly are that!" Arnold responded, not realizing how to be sensitive about his feelings, especially coming from an armadillo. The squonk burst into tears again at Arnold's comment, but Arnold quickly added, "You have to stop crying! Your tears will lead them right to you!"

"I'm so sad, I cannot stop. Crying is what a squonk does," he said.

With this Arnold was about to try to comfort him with words of reassurance when out from behind the squonk jumped a giant, red, barbarian looking man with a club and a large burlap sack. He leapt out and scooped up the squonk in one fell swoop!

"Gotcha!" he shouted, and then laughed in a terrible way.

"No!" Arnold shouted, but he could do nothing about it.

The huge, bright red skinned hunter left and Arnold began to follow the crying which was coming from the sack. But then, suddenly the crying stopped and so did the hunter. He placed the bag down on the ground and opened it, and there was nothing inside but a pool of tears. The giant hunter grew angry, raised his club up high and launched after Arnold who took off deeper into the forest at high speed.

"I may not be great looking, but I don't cry like a squonk, and you won't catch me!" he called out to the hunter.

Soon it was clear that Arnold had gotten away. He had run hard into the woods for some time before he realized that he was so far into the woods, he was lost. He walked carefully on for some time before finally coming to a clearing in the middle of the woods.

"Otto!" Arnold called, as he saw his friend, still dressed in those colorful clothes, waiting for him next to a large green dragon! The dragon had a friendly face and look about him, and wings which spread out from end to end of the clearing.

"Climb aboard my friend!" Otto invited. "We're about to take off!"

Arnold was shown to a lovely cushioned seat inside the

dragon's mouth. The seat was more like a throne, plated in gold trim and resting on the dragon's tongue, which seemed like the softest, warmest red carpet you can imagine. Otto climbed aboard and shouted, "Flip!" and the dragon took off in the air!

Part III: Dawn Breaks

The flight from inside the dragon's mouth was incredible. Never before had Arnold felt so adventurous and safe at the same time. Even though it was still dark, they flew so high as to see the stars like never before. Without any city lights to shield them, they all looked like bright pin pricks in the sky. There were thousands and thousands of twinkling and shooting stars that seemed to dance in the sky. Then they flew back down toward the ground and over the tops of wonderful mountains and trees and finally over a small village which was lit by oil lamplight. It was a romantic old village, straight out of the history books.

They landed on the edge of the village and Arnold walked out from the giant dragon's mouth and onto the street.

"Here you go, Arnold!" announced Otto as if Arnold should know where he was and why he was there.

"Where am I?" Arnold asked. But before he could get an answer he heard a loud call for help coming from a field just outside of the village. When Arnold turned around to ask Otto whether or not they should go and help the person, both he and the dragon had vanished. Arnold was alone.

But when he turned back toward the village, he noticed that all the houses had suddenly leaped off their foundation and were dancing around in excitement. They were happy to see Arnold and he heard their voices proclaim that he had arrived. But Arnold wasn't used to seeing houses with wooden legs dancing around the streets and celebrating, so he was a bit nervous and began to wonder what he was going to do.

"Help! Please, help!" called the voice again. It sounded like a young boy in trouble, and it reminded Arnold of Andy, so he took off right away to help whoever it was leaving behind the dancing houses who seemed not to notice his departure.

Just outside the village he found the young boy who was standing in the middle of a field next to a nice tall cherry tree.

"I'm here, I'm here!" Arnold cried, "Are you in need of help?" he asked.

"Yes! I need your help, I'm so glad you're here," the boy said.

"You don't look hurt or anything. What is the problem?" Arnold asked.

"I must cut this tree down, and I can't seem to do it on my own" the boy said.

"Why do you need to cut this tree down? It looks so lovely! And I love cherries!" Arnold said.

"You can't eat them when they are on the tree, now can you?" the boy asked with a sort of devious smile on his face. It was clear that he wanted to eat cherries too.

"No, I suppose you can't." Arnold said, trying to understand why this still seemed like the wrong way to go about getting the cherries.

"Here, grab the end of this ax and help me swing it!" the boy ordered. He seemed like a natural leader.

With Arnold's help, the boy managed to lift the ax over his shoulder, bringing it down and around in a huge, powerful swing toward the cherry tree's trunk. As it hit the trunk, a loud "CRACK!" was heard and the tree tumbled down to the ground.

"Cherries!" cried Arnold in excitement. It was the first time he thought about food in a long time, and he was missing it.

"What's going on out there?" shouted a grown up man's voice. It came from just beyond the wall at the edge of the field. Whoever it was, he sounded mad.

"It's my father!" the boy shouted.

"Should we run away?" Arnold asked.

"No, there is no place to go. Besides, I think he likes cherries too," the boy insisted.

"George! What happened to my cherry tree!" his father yelled upon reaching them. "Did this armadillo knock it down?" he asked angrily pointing at Arnold.

"I cannot lie, father. No, I cut it down with that ax. He only helped me because I asked him to," the boy admitted.

"We'll see," the man said, still seething with anger. "Into the house with you! And you, you little armadillo, will come with me."

The man grabbed Arnold and walked him into town. The houses there quickly stopped dancing around and resumed their normal places. The man walked into the building whose sign said, "Court House" and proceeded to place Arnold upon a chair in front of a judge.

At first, Arnold was terrified! The judge's bench was huge and very intimidating. But then he suddenly felt relief when he looked up at the judge himself and saw Otto! He was still dressed in his green and red suit, and still chewing on that half smoked cigar. His face still glowed with a greenish blue color. Arnold expected to be freed in a moment, and hoped Otto would take him away again with the dragon. He missed Irene, and wanted to see her again soon.

George's father began to outline the crime Arnold had committed by helping his son destroy his glorious cherry tree by cutting it down right in his very own garden. The judge, Otto, listened intently and without even letting Arnold talk in his own defense, slammed down his gavel and declared,

"Arnold, you are guilty! That's not history!"

"History?" Arnold asked. "What do you mean?"

"It's not how history was supposed to happen. Young George was to cut that tree down on his own, not with the help of an armadillo!"

"You mean, George *Washington?*" Arnold asked, remembering several stories Ellen and Andy had told him ever since his arrival from under the garden wall.

"Arnold," Otto concluded, "I hereby sentence you to be good and true, be brave. And by all means, don't wake up!"

With that he slammed his gavel down and Arnold closed his eyes in fear. He was then led outside and into the forest, which was now completely covered in fresh white snow and ice. It was a wonderfully beautiful place – cool and refreshing. He had never seen snow before and the way it glistened on the trees was breathtaking! Arnold was certainly enjoying this adventure, but he started to wonder when it would end, and how he'd find his way home again. He also thought about Irene and hoped he'd be able to get back to find her soon.

He made his way through the forest and came to what appeared to be a wall of pine trees blocking his way. He pushed through the soft branches for a while and then popped out the other side and onto a city street. He looked around and saw that he was in the middle of a giant city! The entire forest seemed tiny by comparison. The buildings shot up from the ground to heights he had never seen before! He looked up until his neck hurt, and wondered what a tiny little armadillo like him would possible do in a giant city like this, except get lost.

Just then, Arnold noticed the moon in the sky turning around and getting larger. It looked as if it were coming down from the sky after him. As the yellowish looking moon turned around, it had a face that sneered at him. Arnold ran into the city to get away from the moon, which continued to grow in the sky. But the city was too large and complex for him and he didn't know where to go.

As if by sheer will alone, Arnold began to grow larger and larger, and the city grew smaller and smaller all around him. Soon, he was so large that he was able to climb over the tallest of buildings and make his way rapidly across the city. He was very careful to not destroy everything he ran into, but he couldn't help but smash and crush some buildings he walked by. His tail knocked around cars and toppled street signs left and right. But Arnold continued to run away from the moon, which kept growing larger and coming closer in the night sky.

Finally, Arnold could see across to the edge of the city and into another forest. He leapt toward it and continued to run, using all his armadillo instincts to escape the terrifying moon! Just as he approached the edge of the forest, the face of a giant lifted itself out from the street and let out an enormous puff of air that flung Arnold high up into the sky!

Fortunately, Arnold landed on a gigantic mushroom, as tall as a house! He was happy to have landed on such a soft mushroom, but now he didn't know how he would climb down to the ground. Just then he heard the princess's voice!

"Arnold! Arnold!" she shouted, "Down here! Slide!"

Arnold was so happy to hear Irene's voice again that he wasted no time and slid down the side of the mushroom and flew off the edge up into the air, just like his slide at home! He landed on a soft cushion inside an elaborate, beautiful royal carriage and right next to the armadillo he loved! Arnold was never happier!

"Let's go!" Irene called out to the six Imps who were pulling the carriage. The Imps looked a little like court jesters, but to Arnold they reminded him more of circus clowns. They were dressed in skintight clothes with different colors of stars all over. The background was black on one side, white on the other. Their hats had five or six points each dangling down aside their heads with jangling stars dangling from the end of each point. They were happy, but bumbling around as if they were brainless. Arnold found them very fun to watch, and yet they seemed concerned.

"Why are they so worried about getting to the palace on time?" Arnold asked.

"We must get back to Slumberland before dawn. Once the sun comes up, we won't be able to return!" Irene answered, her voice now getting more worried. Arnold looked toward the edge of the sky and noticed the dim glow of what was soon to be the rising sun. Morning was on its way, and the Imps were hustling to make it back in time. Arnold remembered what Otto had said before, "Be good and true, be brave. And by all means, don't wake up!" Now Arnold felt a pit in his stomach. What would happen if they didn't make it?

Just then, as strange as it may sound, they saw a monkey on the back of a flying kangaroo! They flew down next to the carriage and shouted out a warning to the Princess and the Imps that the sun was about to rise! Then, they took back off into the air swiftly as only a monkey riding on the back of a flying kangaroo can do.

The Imps now grew more frantic and each started to struggle with their emotions. They feared the daylight and grew more panicked. They began to pull in different directions and to argue among themselves as to which way is fastest. The result was that the carriage came to a complete stop.

Princess Irene then noticed a couple of giant balls

resting off to the side of the road, and just beyond them were the cannon the soldiers had used to fire them toward the palace.

"We can use those cannon balls!" she proclaimed with excitement.

"What do you mean?" Arnold asked.

"Come on! Climb inside one of the balls, and we'll have the Imps fire us into the palace before the sunrise!" Irene answered.

It seemed like a crazy idea, but after all he had been through, somehow he was able to make sense of this plan and chased after Irene who had already made her way over to a cannonball.

The two armadillos got inside their cannonballs, and the Imps proceeded to load them into the cannons. With a short countdown to zero, they were both blasted up into the air toward the palace!

Arnold felt like he had just been flung so hard into the air that he might reach the moon! But then it was all quiet and calm and he felt as if he was weightless, floating in the air. But he braced himself for the impact that would mean landing! He curled up into a ball as tightly as he could and squeezed his eyes shut waiting for the moment when he would crash! He prayed he would survive, but now he wasn't so sure. Suddenly, a strange feeling came over him as if he was losing his grip on himself. His hands and feet were struggling to hold onto his own body, and he felt the incredible urge to burst out from the cannonball itself as if he was a firework ready to explode! Then, all of the sudden, he did just that! POP! BANG! *BOOM!*

125

"Ahhh!!!" The scream had clearly come from the Fort! Ellen and Andy ran out to check on Arnold.

"What's the matter Arnold?" asked Andy who was out of breath when he arrived.

Arnold finally opened his eyes and looked around. He had fallen out of his bed and onto the floor.

"I popped!" Arnold said, still stunned.

"You popped?" Andy asked.

"Yes. I popped. I was a firework and I popped in the sky," Arnold explained. Then he realized that the sun was shining brightly in the sky, and it was morning.

"You were only dreaming, silly!" Ellen reassured him. "Must have been quite exciting! You're all sweaty!"

"Irene?" Arnold cried. "Where is she?"

"Just relax for a while Arnold," Ellen said. "We're leaving for grandma and grandpa's house now, but we'll be back tomorrow. Go play with Henry and Boomer!"

"But maybe you shouldn't eat any more human food for a while," Andy said.

"I guess eating so much before bedtime gives him nightmares." Ellen said to Andy as they walked back toward the house.

Arnold sat there for a while, feeling horrible. But this time it wasn't because he was sick from the food. It was because he had realized that Irene was nothing more than a dream.

"Dreams don't last very long at all," he said to himself, "They aren't real, and they never come true." A moment later, he began to cry.

"Hang in there, Arnold," A voice called him from

behind.

Arnold looked up and saw Henry sitting quietly in the corner.

"I heard your scream and came over to check on you. You have a lot of friends you know. Even Penni was looking over from Mrs. Widmer's house to make sure you were okay."

"Thank you, Henry," Arnold said.

"You had a great adventure in your dream, and you saw Irene again?" Henry asked.

"Yes," Arnold said sadly.

"Well, it's okay to feel sad that she's gone. Losing someone is not easy. But it's not the end of the story either. You never know how things will end eventually," Henry reassured.

"Sometimes I just don't believe in anything anymore. It's just not fair," Arnold said, wiping more tears from his eyes.

"No, it's not fair," said Henry. "But you'll find your happiness again, Arnold, because you own your own heart. Giving it to someone is the most special thing you can ever do, but it's always yours and no one can ever take that away from you."

Chapter 8

The Adventure of a
Huckleberry Armadillo

Otto had become one of the family, more or less, and was now allowed inside Ellen and Andy's house. He had learned to open the back door all by himself by jumping high enough to reach and pull down on the handle. He was always careful to shut the door behind him as well. The kid's father would laugh every time Otto showed up, because he had no idea how that cat would be able to come and go as he pleased!

"We don't have a kitty hole in our doors here," he said. "How does he get in? Are you kids letting him in?"

"No!" Ellen would answer. "We've been sitting here the whole time." And then all three of them would laugh out loud and take turns petting Otto.

"He has to be the smartest cat I've ever seen" Dad would say as he got up to inspect the doors only to find that they were all closed.

One time, he even saw the kitchen light go off and then Otto proudly walked into the living room. It was almost as if Otto was saying, "You shouldn't leave the lights on in a room you're not using," as he managed to leap up and switch them off.

Then one day he heard their Dad tell the kids to be on the lookout for a little lost puppy. He had seen a small sign posted on a telephone pole as he drove into their neighborhood which read, "Lost puppy, small, big eyes, rags." He said that the sign looked as if a child had made it, and he didn't know what "rags" meant as far as describing a dog, other than it must be an ugly dog.

Never able to turn away from a mystery, Otto called on his friends Arnold and Henry to meet the next morning out front to discuss the mystery. He had invited Boomer as well, who said he would be there, but as usual, he was not. So once Ellen and Andy left for school, the three of them made their way to the Bakers where they found Boomer still asleep. They woke him, and began to talk about the missing puppy.

"If I ran away, I would be hiding in Mrs. Widmer's yard." Arnold said, "That is the last place someone would dare to go looking."

"Except for Mrs. Widmer!" Henry added. "She'd find you, or Penni would, and then she'd scream her head off! So, I think we can assume the puppy didn't go there."

"An excellent deduction, Henry," Otto said.

"You actually woke me up, for this?" Boomer complained in his slow and dramatic, deep voice.

"Well, did you see or hear anything?" Arnold asked.

"What?" Boomer replied.

"Did you see, or hear anything?" Arnold asked in a louder voice.

"What did you say?" Boomer squinted and asked again.

"Did you see anything? Did you hear anything?" Arnold shouted at Boomer, who just grinned.

"Really? You're asking me?" Boomer smirked, then laid his head back down and promptly fell asleep.

Arnold was annoyed that Boomer had tricked him like that, so he mumbled under his breath, "Wish I had some bacon to eat right in front of him."

"Bacon?" Boomer said as his head immediately shot up in excitement from his slumber. Everyone laughed, and Arnold proudly smirked back at Boomer who looked at him in disgust, and laid his head back down.

"Listen, we don't know if the puppy ran away, or if someone took him." Otto explained. "I suggest we split up this morning and go look for clues."

"What kind of clues are we looking for?" asked Henry. Henry was always a good one to ask a lot of questions.

"Anything that might help us to find out what happened. Another "missing" poster, footprints, fresh little doggie poo, anything." Otto said.

"Doggie poo?" Arnold asked, looking rather disgusted.

"Yes!" Otto explained. "That is a sure sign that the pup was there and there recently! A little doggie poo poo would be absolutely fantastic right now!" Otto explained in an excited tone of voice.

"Why don't you go have some for breakfast?" Boomer mumbled, his cheek flapping gently against the ground as he spoke, "And leave me alone."

But just as they began to move out from the meeting to begin their search, Otto added "and don't forget to look in the pools and the creek for a body."

With that comment, everyone froze and the lighthearted nature of the conversation suddenly ended.

"Body?" Arnold asked shyly.

"Yes, body." Otto repeated in a matter of fact tone. "He may have slipped into a pool at night and drowned. Or he distance, thinking. Then, after a long pause he looked toward the others who were still somewhat in shock about what he had just said. "Anything is possible, we need to check everything. On your way!" he ordered. "And Arnold, don't lose your glasses. You need them to look sharp for clues." Arnold nodded in agreement and checked to make sure his glasses were secure.

With that, the group split up with Otto heading north toward Canterbury Park, Henry set to explore the woods off to the east, and Arnold heading toward the south part of the neighborhood down toward Marwood Creek.

It wasn't long before Arnold came across Huck, a little boy who lived down at the end of the block. Huck was only about four years old so he didn't go to school yet. He lived several houses up the road from Ellen and Andy. His clothes were typically very old, bought mainly from garage sales or donation stores, and he looked as though he had never even seen a bathtub. He was an only child, and wandered around the neighborhood more or less on his own and without a care in the world.

Huck loved to be outside most of the time. He spent hours wandering up and down the streets of the neighborhood, picking up sticks and waving them in the air as if they were swords, placing stones together into little houses, or even playing hide-and-seek with himself. Although he looked happy, he seemed like a very lonely little boy. And while the other kids in the neighborhood took to calling him "Rags" because of how he dressed in dirty, raggedy old clothes, Arnold liked him. If he were eating something, Huck would always offer to share it with Arnold. And Arnold would listen to Huck telling him amazing stories of adventures he had, even though they were only make-believe. After a while, Arnold began to wonder if Huck had any parents at all, or anyone to care for him. And although he smelled grubby, to Arnold that wasn't a bad thing.

Huck was out again this morning, alone, playing some sort of hide-and-seek game near his house. Arnold saw him crawling into the bushes in his front yard, and then back out again. He saw him repeat this a few times before moving in closer to talk to the little boy.

"Huck? What are you doing?" Arnold asked. For some reason Huck didn't seem surprised that an armadillo was talking to him. He was more surprised that an armadillo was standing there wearing a pair of glasses! He had seen Arnold before, but he never noticed his glasses.

"Let me try!" Huck said with a little excitement in his voice as he reached over to take Arnold's glasses.

"No! Those are my glasses, Huck. You mustn't touch them, please!" Arnold moved away quickly. But Huck was a curious little boy and he saw that getting Arnold's glasses might be more fun if he had to chase Arnold around. So he quickly started to run around the bushes, chasing Arnold who seemed more than a little concerned!

"Huck! Stop! I can't run around here in this circle forever! I'm getting dizzy!" Arnold shouted. But Huck just laughed and giggled and continued to chase Arnold. Soon Huck quickly fell behind Arnold who, without realizing it, actually caught back up to Huck and was now, in fact, chasing him around the bushes!

Very dizzy, and quite dazed and tired, Arnold suddenly veered off and ran smack dab into a large oak three which stood in the middle of the bushes. He hit the tree so hard that his glasses flew off as he sputtered backward onto his butt! Arnold was left there sitting down in between the bushes, shaking his head, and seeing stars floating around him.

Just then, a loud snappy bark echoed out from under the bushes. "Huh? What was that?" Arnold thought, unable to speak without his glasses. He began to feel around for his glasses but kept running into sticks and brush. He was beginning to panic about finding them when he heard the high little bark again.

The barking continued and it sounded like it was very, very close. Arnold sniffed around and followed the sound. Within just a few feet, he came upon a cute, tiny little puppy. He was wagging his short little stump of a tail as hard as he could and was very excited because he was standing right next to Arnold's glasses. Arnold squinted hard to try to focus his eyes and see the puppy, but he couldn't quite make it out, even though he was less than a foot from him. Finally, Huck pushed his way through the bushes and picked up the puppy.

"Oh, my little baby pup!" Huck said as he cuddled the puppy.

Arnold took another step forward and found his glasses. He placed them upon his head and regained his sight, and ability to communicate.

"Huck! Is that your puppy?" Arnold asked.

"Yes! He's mine!" Huck answered, and seemed very concerned.

"He's very cute! Does he have a name?" Arnold asked.

"I call him, Rags" Huck answered. "He's my bestest friend in the whole wide world," Huck gave him a very big hug and held him close to his chest.

"Hi Rags!" said Arnold. "My name is Arnold."

Rags only barked back. He was just a puppy, and hadn't learned how to talk yet.

"I didn't know you had a puppy Huck. When did you get him?" Arnold asked, realizing that this was probably the puppy for which he and his friends were looking.

"I found him, and I am keeping him. My mommy says I have to give him away. But I won't give him away. I found him and he's mine." Huck finished.

"But his owner, I mean, someone else might be missing him too." Arnold said.

"I'm keeping him!" Huck answered, growing angry.

"Well, people will come looking for him soon. And your mommy will want you to go inside soon too." Arnold explained, hoping Huck would understand and allow the puppy to go with him back to Ellen and Andy's house so they could help him get back to his real home.

"No!" Huck began to cry. "He's mine, I love him, he's my friend! He's my only friend in the world!" Huck fell to the ground in tears. Rags looked up at him and quickly started to lick his tears away, and soon he was making Huck giggle. "Hey, that tickles!" Huck said as he picked Rags back up and hugged him once again.

The more he watched, the more Arnold felt sorry for Huck. He was being teased when some of the older kids in the neighborhood called him "rags" but he didn't seem to understand that it was an insult. Instead, he went and named his beloved puppy "Rags." Arnold didn't have the heart to try to convince Huck to give up the puppy. Instead, he simply warned Huck.

Rags

"What are you going to do when they come looking for him?" Arnold asked.

"I will run away." Huck answered.

"Where? They will catch you. You're not that fast, even I caught up to you!" Arnold explained.

"I have a boat, see!" Huck pointed over toward his backyard and began to walk in that direction. Arnold followed as Huck led him down toward Marwood Creek which ran through the neighborhood. In the creek was tied a little wooden boat, just big enough for a small boy.

"I am going to float away down the river and live with Rags." Huck explained. His plan didn't seem too well thought out, and Arnold worried that he'd get in trouble, or tip over and drown. So he decided to offer his help in running away down the creek, thinking it probably wouldn't last too long before someone would come looking for them.

"Maybe I can come with you, Huck." Arnold said. "I think you might need some help."

"You promise not to tell anyone?" Huck asked.

Arnold paused to think about it. He knew helping Huck run away was probably not the right thing to do. But neither was giving up his cute little puppy, Rags. As Arnold continued to think about it, Rags gave a little bark as if to say, "Please?"

"Okay, I promise." Arnold said.

"Yay!" Huck shouted, and Rags let out a few more cheerful barks.

The three of them carefully crawled into the boat and cast off for a destination unknown. They managed to escape unnoticed, and soon found themselves enjoying a nice, slow ride down Marwood Creek into parts of the neighborhood they had never seen before.

Part II: The Duke and the King

It wasn't long before the three friends reached a small man-made waterfall. There were two large rocks, one on either side of the creek which was about five feet wide at that point. The water fall was only a couple of feet, just enough to be decorative for whoever lived in the fancy house through whose backyard the creek flowed. On each rock was a boy around twelve years old, each holding a large stick or branch, and playing some sort of game.

"Tis me sir! I have stolen the maiden and she shan't be returned!" shouted one boy to the other. He then leaped across the creek from one rock onto the other, and engaged his foe in a sword fight which seemed fairly exciting to Arnold, as well as intimidating.

"Wait! Stop!" the second boy said as the little boat came into view, "What have we here?"

The boys reached out and grabbed the bow of the boat and pulled it next to the creek's edge.

"You can't go over that waterfall," the first boy said, "It's far too dangerous!" he finished with an exaggerated tone which made it sound much more dangerous than it really was.

"What is this?" the other boy asked, "a little dog and an armadillo too?" The boys laughed at the site of Huck, little Rags, and an armadillo wearing thick glasses!

"I don't see what's so funny," Arnold spoke up.

"Wow! Did you hear that?" the first boy said.

"Yeah! Do it again!" the second boy said.

"Do what again?" Arnold asked.

"Yes! It was real!" the second boy said. "I don't believe

it! He talked!"

"Yeah, he did, didn't he?" said the first boy who looked as though he was solving a puzzle, rubbing his chin with his hand and thinking. "I have an idea!" he said as a sly smile came across his face.

"Allow me to introduce myself, gents!" the first boy continued. "My name is Duke."

"Duke?" asked Huck.

"Yes, Duke." Duke answered, "And this is King, ah... King..." he couldn't think of a proper name, so he finally said, "Just King. Yes, but you can call him "Your Majesty."

"You mean, you're a real King?" asked Huck who was now in awe of these older boys who seemed so wise and powerful.

"Of course!" Duke said. "And I am a real Duke. Now then, since you are floating on our river, what have you brought for us?"

"Yeah!" King chimed in, "We require a toll before you can pass!" he said with an evil laugh.

"Toll?" Huck asked. "What do you mean?"

"If you want to sail safely down this creek, my friend, you'll need to pay up! After all, this is royal property you're on, and you must pay a tax to the King for all the protection he provides!" said the Duke with his large, sly smile.

"But I don't have any money." Huck answered.

"Oh yes, now that is a problem, isn't it?" replied the Duke. "But I think I can help you out there. What I'll do for you is borrow your little armadillo friend here. Then I'll send you safely over this waterfall and down the creek as you desire!" the Duke said, looking shrewdly at Arnold.

Huck hesitated. He was only four, and he was a bit scared.

"I promise we won't hurt him! In fact, we'll take good care of the little armadillo! After all, a talking armadillo is going to be worth millions!" the Duke revealed.

"No, I want to keep my friends with me." Huck said.

"Well now, you should! Yes, indeed, you should want to keep your friends. If they are true friends that is. If not, then getting rid of them is really the best thing you can do. No one wants someone who will stab you in the back when times get rough now, do they? And this little armadillo will go off and become famous, and leave you behind little boy. Now, do you think he's really a good friend?"

"But I am his friend!" Arnold shouted angrily.

"Shhh!" the King commanded of Arnold. "Be quiet, it is not your turn to speak!"

"Friends are very delicate things." The Duke continued, now bending down close to Huck's ear and speaking softly. "They will never last when one of them sees an easier way to go. They will always betray you and disappoint you at some point. They may even say that they love you, but don't believe it. No, even your best friend in the world will leave you eventually. But your King must care for you forever. It is his divine right, his sacred duty! He will never abandon you. So, if you help make your King rich, he will help you to do whatever you want!"

"You mean, I can keep my puppy, Rags?" Huck said excitedly.

"Of course!" the Duke looked down into the boat and

noticed little Rags, hiding and shivering under Huck's feet.

"Ah, just a moment please!" said Arnold. "I'm not too sure about this. In fact, I think you're not a real Duke, or King at all. I think you should be in school just like Ellen and Andy."

"School?" answered the Duke. "Only the King tells you when you must go to school. Do I have to go to school today, King?" the Duke turned and asked.

"No school today!" replied the King.

"You see! No school today." The Duke answered with a smile. "It's just that easy." Then, turning back to Huck he said, "So, just hand him over to us and you'll be on your way."

"Hand him over?" Huck asked.

"Yes. Give him to me!" the Duke demanded.

It suddenly dawned on Huck what they intended to do was to steal Arnold and send him away. They were just a couple of swindlers trying to bully him, and he grew defiant instead.

"No! Never!" Huck shouted. "Leave us alone!"
"Hand him over you idiot!" the Duke leaned over into the boat and tried to grab Arnold by force. But Arnold dodged him by moving to the back of the boat which tipped violently as the Duke slipped onto its edge and caused it to bob up and down in the water.

It was a mad scramble as the Duke tried over and over to grab Arnold who managed to squirm around inside the boat and escape being captured while Huck and Rags held on for dear life as the boat rocked up and down violently.

Finally, Rags gave out a loud piercing little bark and snapped at the Duke's hand as it was near the bottom of the inside of the boat.

"Ouch!" cried the Duke as he stood up, out of breath, and very angry. "Fine!" he shouted. "If you won't give us that stupid armadillo, we'll just take your stupid little dog!" and he reached into the boat and grabbed Rags by the scruff of his neck and pulled him swiftly out of the boat. The Duke held him up in the air like a trophy while the King clapped his hands with pride.

"Give him back!" screamed Huck with tears in his eyes.

"Never!" shouted the Duke in return. "You had your chance, so now shove off!" The Duke placed his foot onto the edge of the boat and pushed it hard off shore and into the creek. The boat turned sideways as it headed down toward the waterfall just a few feet away. Because of this, the boat got caught between the rocks instead of floating over the little waterfall. Rags kept barking and whimpering, but the boys simply laughed at him and at Huck who was now sitting in his boat, stuck at the top of the waterfall.

Seeing a chance to have some more fun, the Duke approached the boat and challenged Huck.

"If you can get out, climb on that rock, and then leap across to the rock on this side of the creek, I'll give you your dog back."

"Don't do it." Arnold said to Huck. "They are liars, and you'll fall in the creek."

But Huck didn't listen. He loved Rags and couldn't stand to see him in the arms of these bullies – he imagined the mean things they would do to his puppy. So he carefully stood up in the boat, and managed to make his way out and onto the rock on the far side of the creek. The boys, and Arnold, all watched in anticipation, holding their breath. Huck stood up on the rock, and looked across at the other side. It seemed impossible to jump across the water that far.

"Do it!" shouted the King. "Do it you grubby little boy! Or are you too scared?" he taunted.

"Come on, we haven't got all day" the Duke said.

"Actually, with no school, we do," the King replied and then they both laughed.

Arnold knew Huck was being set up, and he tried to think of something they could do to escape, but nothing was coming to mind. Finally, Huck jumped! But as expected, he didn't get far. It was almost as if he hadn't jumped at all as he landed square onto the top of the waterfall and rolled down it into the creek below with a big splash!

The Duke and the King began to laugh their heads off, rolling around on the ground, unable to contain themselves. Huck stood up and waded over to the edge of the shallow creek on the opposite side from the boys, scared and ashamed. The Duke and the King began to call Huck various names as they laughed at him, all the while holding onto
Rags who looked very scared and confused.

Arnold had had enough and became determined to do something in order to get the puppy back. And then, he had what he thought was a fantastic idea.

"Excuse me, ah, King and Duke Sirs!" Arnold shouted

above their laughter. "I don't think you're royalty at all. I think you are just a couple of human kids who are very good at picking on others so you can feel good about yourself. You really can't do much on your own, now can you?"

The boys stood up silently, and stared over at Arnold. Arnold took a deep breath and swallowed what felt like a giant lump in his throat. He had never really stood up to anyone before, and certainly never tried to provoke anyone. But he remembered what Ellen and Andy had told him which was that the only way to deal with a bully is to stand up to him. Arnold was trying to stand up to two of them.

"You said something?" the Duke said, as if he was daring Arnold to say it again.

"Yes," Arnold said slowly, "I said you don't amount to very much, do you? I mean, you probably don't do well in school, have only each other as a friend, and perhaps you can't even jump across the creek like you asked Huck to do."

"Oh yeah?" the King answered. "We can jump the creek, no problem!"

"Really?" Arnold said. "That would be impressive. Could I see you do it?"

The Duke thought for a moment. Perhaps it was a trick? But then he realized he was dealing with an armadillo – how smart can it be? "Okay, stand back." He said as he moved over toward one of the rocks which made up the top of the waterfall. He looked around and down at the cascading water falling smoothly over the edge below him.

Then he looked straight up at Arnold, and leaped across from one rock to the other without even looking down. He smiled wryly back at Arnold, proud of his achievement.

"Ha!" shouted the King, still on his side of the creek. "See, you're just a stupid little animal! Why don't you go bury some acorns or something!" he laughed.

"I am an armadillo, not a squirrel. I don't bury acorns." Arnold said, calmly correcting the King. "But if you're truly a King, and you a Duke, then surly you could cross over the creek at the same time, while also walking onto this boat to get across."

"To you little squirrel, I am a King! And you will learn to show me some respect!" the King announced, trying to antagonize Arnold.

"Fine." Said the Duke, who began to move back toward the creek. "But if we make it across, then you come with us as well! We can definitely use a talking armadillo! I have a cage that's just right for you and a mean old dog for a friend!" he said laughing.

"Agreed" said Arnold, now hoping more than ever that his plan would work. It wasn't much of a plan, and he remembered that usually his ideas did more to get him into trouble than to succeed. Oh, he wished Otto was there to help him think things through, but now there was no going back.

The two boys were on opposite sides of the creek and moved toward the boat, the Duke still carrying Rags with him. Slowly, knowing they would need to carefully balance themselves with each step as they crossed the rocking boat, they each placed a foot onto opposite sides of it in

146

order to balance. The boat rocked suddenly and both boys tipped a little, but regained their balance.

"Don't you tip me over!" the Duke warned the King sternly.

"I won't if you won't." the King replied.

By now both boys had a slight look of worry. They made a second step toward each other and again the boat rocked suddenly and violently. But both boys managed to keep their balance. Now they were face to face and the next step would require them to pass each other on the tiny little rowboat.

"Place your foot over there when I say go" ordered the Duke. Then he began to count. "One, two, three!"

On three they both moved their feet toward opposite sides of the boat, but they also bumped into each other and the boat began to rock back and forth with incredible speed! They grabbed each other in a bear hug in order to try to regain their balance and not topple over into the water. It was at this moment that Arnold put his plan into action! He jumped up from one side of the boat over to the other side, placing all of his weight toward the waterfall with the hope of tipping the boat over just enough to cause the boys to fall in the water. But just as he made his leap, the boat stopped rocking entirely.

"Ha, ha!" shouted the King. "We made it!"

The boys had managed to stabilize the boat and were now turned around but still facing each other. The Duke looked sharply down at Arnold and sneered. "You'll pay for that, little one!"

Arnold swallowed hard once again, and began to dread

that he ever tried to help Huck and Rags run away. He felt like he let his new friends down. He was convinced that nothing he did would ever work out as he hoped. And this time, he allowed two friends to get into trouble as well.

But just then a loud man's voice sharply ripped through the air. "Hey there! What are you kids doing?"

The shout startled the kids who were obviously not supposed to be playing around the creek in someone else's backyard. The boat began to rock back and forth like crazy once again, and the boys were very close to tipping over. They managed to hold onto each other just enough to begin stabilizing the boat once again when Arnold leaped across the boat one more time, pushing down on the other side just enough to force the boat to rock again! The boys both shouted out in panic as they overcompensated by lunging over to the waterfall side of the boat. They immediately toppled over the side and fell straight down the small waterfall and splashed into the creek!

Arnold was thrilled and Huck shouted and clapped from the far side of the creek. But that's when they noticed a loud, sharp little bark calling to them. The Duke had still been holding Rags and he had fallen into the creek with him. Now, the little puppy was floating away down the river, struggling to keep his little head above the water.

"Rags!" shouted as he ran after him down the side of the creek.

"Oh no! What have I done?" Arnold looked on from the boat, still lodged above the waterfall between the two rocks. He couldn't swim, and even if he could, he was stuck where he was! All he could do was watch in horror as little Rags slipped down the creek with little Huck chasing after in terror.

Arnold adjusted his glasses and then saw from where the loud man's voice had come. A tall man was standing next to the creek about fifty yards away. Seeing all the commotion, he wandered down to the edge of the creek, reached over and lifted little Rags out of the stream. He didn't appear exactly to be a caring man, for he just held the puppy by the scruff of his neck down by his side as if he were like a tiny suitcase. Huck stopped running on the opposite side of the creek and stood looking at the man, he had tears in his eyes.

"You kids get out of here!" the man shouted sternly toward the Duke and the King, who managed to climb out of the creek soaking wet, and ran off.

"What are you doing here anyway?" the man snapped at Huck.

"That's my puppy. I want my puppy!" Huck began to cry. All the excitement was simply too much for him.

"Well, I don't see any tags on this little thing." The man said as he held Rags up in front of his eyes to take a look. "He's not yours to keep. You're a little kid. Where are your parents? Where do you live?"

Huck was unable to answer since he was so upset and it sounded as if the man was yelling at him.

"Go home little boy! I'll take care of this pup," snapped the man. He then turned and walked back up toward a building with Rags in his right hand, swinging along as if he were holding a baseball down by his side.

"Rags!" cried Huck. A little sharp bark returned the call, and then the man and Rags disappeared behind a brick wall. The sound of a metal cage was heard being opened and shut again and with it several other dogs and animals could be heard barking from in and around the building.

Part III: Escape from Rex

"Keep a close eye on this little one, Rex." The man said as he dropped Rags into the cage. "Show him the ropes, boy!" Rex was named after the T-Rex dinosaur because he had large sharp teeth and a terrible disposition. He walked outside a series of cages as if he ran the place, which in fact, he did. He kept all the other animals there in line, obeying his directions, and staying put until their owners picked them up. He was the guard dog for the kennel, and the building the man walked into was his office. He was a veterinarian and the kennel was inside a large walled off space outside and next to the main building. There was a door from inside the building that led directly into the kennel, and the outside gate, which had a lock. Even if they could get past the lock, Arnold and Huck would still need to go through Rex and his vicious set of sharp teeth, to reach Rags.

The Vet often acted as if he had no heart at all. He pricked the animals with needles and shots, drawing blood and injecting them with medicine. He laughed loudly when it was over, then saying to the dog, with a fake smile, "Now that wasn't so bad, was it?" But it was! Every animal in town knew about "the Vet" and even Rags, as young as he was, remembered Huck's mother telling them that it was either give him away or take him to "the Vet." Now, he shivered in utter fear at what was to come.

The man walked inside his office as Rex snapped loudly at Rags who cringed into the corner of the cage. Rex quickly explained that Rags would eat after he did, and that his meals would amount to leftovers and other scraps. Then he would be walked around but he would never leave the yard. He would bark only when he was told to, and playing games was out of the question. "We have discipline here!" Rex declared. "And anyone who doesn't obey, gets a visit to the doctor!" As he said this, Rex slowly smiled and displayed his evil, large, sharp, bright teeth, with saliva oozing out from between them and dribbling down his cheeks and long gray tongue.

Just off to the side of the building, Huck and Arnold had snuck up to see where Rags had ended up. They saw the cages lined up against a long wall, each containing a dog or cat. There were also several ferrets in the last cage, but they seemed quite content with themselves. Everyone else seemed miserable and scared. Then, through an open window from just above their heads they heard a loud yelp from a puppy dog inside. It cried several times before they heard the Vet's voice say, "Now, that wasn't so bad was it?"

They knew it wouldn't be long before Rags was taken inside to see the Vet for his shots and who knows what other torture. Arnold had heard terrible stories about the Vet from Henry who described an ice-cold stainless steel table on which they placed you. You paws would slip and slide and you looked and felt like a bumbling idiot. Then, they pricked you with a needle, shined bright light in your eyes and made you cough and wheeze by jamming different things into your ears and mouth. You left there feeling worse than ever, and they knew that some animals never left there at all.

Now, Arnold realized where he was, and that he knew he must rescue Rags before it was too late. They continued to listen to the Vet's voice bellowing out from the window again saying, "Let me know when that cat arrives. He's long overdue for his check-up – I'll be looking forward to getting with him again! He scratched me something fierce last time."

"Yes, doctor," replied the nurse, and the two left the room. Arnold and Huck slowly slipped back down toward the creek and away from the building.

"This may be our only chance, Huck!" Arnold said.

"That dog Rex is too scary. He'll bite me if I try to get my puppy out." Huck said as his eyes began to fill with tears.

"You're right, Huck" Arnold continued, "That's why we need a distraction. And the cat he's expecting will be just that."

"What do you mean?" Huck asked.

"I will pretend to be the cat! They will let me into the waiting room and then I can sneak into the kennel and release Rags from the inside!"

"But how are you going to get in?" Huck asked.

"Through the front door when the next person comes." Arnold thought. But even as he spoke about his plan, he already began having doubts that it would work. Just then, a car door slammed shut, and a woman's voice was heard. The two ran to the other side of the Vet's building and saw the parking lot. There, a woman was handing over an animal carrier to the nurse.

"I'll place him right here on the patio until the doctor is ready, it will be a little while. You can pick him up tomorrow." The nurse finished.

The woman returned to her car and drove off.

"Perfect!" Arnold said. "I will let the cat out and take his place! Tonight, I will be inside and I will let Rags go free!" Then Arnold thought about it and added, "I might just let them all go free!"

Arnold slowly approached the animal carrier, which was actually a plastic box with holes in it and a metal cage door. As he looked inside the door, he was shocked and thrilled to see that the cat, which had just been dropped off, was Otto!

"Arnold!" Otto exclaimed. "What are you doing here?" he asked.

"I am so happy to see you, Otto!" Arnold said. "We need your help to rescue Huck's little puppy."

"Get me out of this cage, and help you I will." Otto said.

Otto explained how to open the cage by pushing down on the top corner where the hinge of the cage door attached. The plastic moved just far enough for Otto to dislocate the spring, which kept the door attached. It flung open, and both ran down the drive toward a small group of bushes. Otto noticed a small ketchup packet lying in the parking lot, and proceeded to come up with his own plan to rescue Rags.

Otto explained his plan to Arnold and Huck and each agreed that Otto was a brilliant cat! Otto then took off very carefully, slowly walking up and down and around the building. He was spying on everything, taking notes in his head about the layout and the various animals in the kennel. Most of all, he took note of Rex. He studied Rex for what seemed like an hour, then he climbed down from the kennel wall, and ran back over to Arnold and Huck.

Otto explained to the gang exactly what to do. Huck was to wait by the creek with the boat ready to go. Arnold was to take a position under the porch step, and race into the building after they took Otto inside. Otto would create a panic, and that would be the distraction needed to allow Arnold into the kennel to free Rags.

"But what about Rex?" Arnold worried.

"They will send him outside. Just wait until they do."

"How do you know they will do that?" Arnold asked.

Otto just smiled calmly and said, "Trust me."

They all took up their positions and waited anxiously for the nurse. Otto smeared his neck with the ketchup and lay down on the porch just outside his cage. Then he gave out a

horrible, wild, shrieking scream which was so real sounding that Arnold popped his head up to see if Otto was okay.

"Get down!" Otto demanded in a tense whisper. Arnold quickly ducked his head and waited.

When the nurse stepped outside to see what was the matter, she caught sight of Otto lying there in what she thought was a pool of blood, she let out a terrible scream of her own.

Then she touched Otto, nudging him to see if he was asleep. He didn't move a muscle – not even to take a breath. The Vet came rushing out to see what was the matter and then he saw the cat.

"Oh my lord!" he yelled. "What happened?"

"He must have been attacked! Look, the carrier door was ripped off the hinge!" the nurse shouted in panic.

"Get him inside, quick!" the Vet ordered. "And let Rex out. I'm sure he'll find the beast responsible for this! It could be one of those rabid raccoons or a fox."

The nurse scooped up Otto and proceeded into the building. Just in time, Arnold leaped up and rushed in before the door shut behind them. Once inside, they took Otto into the emergency room, and Arnold peaked into the kennel from the side doorway. Otto had observed that there was a kitty door in it, so all Arnold had to do was poke his head through once Rex was out of the way. Within a few seconds, the nurse had released Rex to go find the beast who they thought had attacked Otto.

Arnold moved through the doorway into the kennel and walked carefully against the wall to Rags' cage. He managed to open the latch of the cage and Rags popped out, jumping up and down and barking with joy! His barks, however, caught the attention of all the other animals that began to bark as well. They all wanted to be freed, and they were all making a lot of noise.

"What's going on out there?" The Vet asked. "And what is with this cat?" He began to notice that something was just not right about this situation. The cat seemed to be unharmed, he wasn't actively bleeding and he couldn't find a wound on his neck. Then he bent over and sniffed the wound and realized that it was actually ketchup and not blood. He stood straight up and said, "Huh?"

In a flash, Otto opened his eyes, looked up at the Vet and said, "Meow!" He smiled and leaped down from the table and tore out the doorway into the waiting room.

"Get him!" the Vet yelled. "Catch that rotten little beast!"

Otto managed to race out into the kennel through the kitty door where he found Arnold and Rags jumping onto the sides of all the cages, hitting the levers that opened them, and letting all the animals go free.

Soon the entire kennel was in utter chaos with dogs, cats, and even the ferrets running around in circles and knocking over water dishes, and tearing up the pillows from their cages leaving feathers flying everywhere! Trashcans used to store food were tipped over and a feast was underway! It was an incredible site of complete destruction of the kennel, and in the middle of it all was a tiny little firecracker of a pup, and a little armadillo who took a chance on caring for someone else.

"They're coming for us, run!" Otto yelled at the group. They all tore through the kennel and out into the backyard.

The Vet appeared right behind Otto and shouted at the top of his lungs, "Stop you rotten little creatures!" Then he shouted out something which put the fear of death into all of them. "REX!!!"

"Arnold! Hit that last can!" Otto ordered as they all ran toward the backyard. Arnold jumped up against the side of the large trash can which began to wobble. Otto leaped up onto the top and pushed himself between the can and the wall, forcing it to tip over. The can fell and poured out a ton of dog and cat poop onto the floor of the kennel just as the Vet was about to run by. He tried to stop and avoid the cascading pile of poop, but his foot caught on a large piece, which obviously had belonged to Rex, causing him to slip and land face down into the pile.

Otto tore out the back door and was the last to make it out into the yard. The Vet looked up, his face covered in poop and shouted once again in a rage of anger, "REX!!!!"

The animals scattered quickly once they found their freedom, and Otto, Arnold, and Rags stopped to look back on what they had done.

"Well done!" Otto said.

Rags barked with joy, and Arnold smiled. But just then, a deep and angry bark barreled across the yard. Rex tore around the corner of the building, spit from his mouth foaming up and flying off in all directions with each stride. He was running at top speed and he was angrier than anyone had ever seen before. It was his job to keep order in the kennel, and he took this prison break personally. He never looked back, he only looked at Otto, rags, and especially Arnold – since he was the only wild animal of the bunch.

"Run." Otto said calmly.

"But Otto, what are you..." Arnold began to argue when Otto interrupted.

"Run! Now!" he shouted.

Arnold and Rags took off for the boat, but it was clear they were not going to make it. Otto tried to run in a different direction in order to draw Rex away from them, but this time his plan didn't work. Rex ignored Otto entirely and shoved him aside as he leaped through the air with a deep and angry growl! He was thirsty for blood! Armadillo blood!

"Run, Rags, run!" Arnold shouted to the little pup that could now see the boat in the distance. Huck began to call Rags on as well. Arnold knew Rex was going to catch one of them, but probably not both. And as scared and frightened as he was, all he wanted was to see Rags make it back into Huck's arms again.

Rex began to bark as he gained ground on them fast. It was as if trains were coming their way and there was no way to avoid it! It was going to hit, and it would be the end for them. But there was still a chance for one to survive. Arnold had been running hard and leading Rags, but now he slowed down and shouted at Rags one more time, "Run to Huck, Rags, run and go home!"

Rags continued on and pulled in front of Arnold! He never looked back as his tiny little legs pounded the ground beneath him and his little bark trailed off toward his little owner, Huck. Rags leaped up into Huck's arms and they both fell back into the little boat, safe and sound and together at last.

But Arnold was now in great peril. He had slowed in order to sacrifice himself and allow Rags to get away, and just as he had made it into the boat, he felt Rex's gigantic paw slap him to the left as if he had ran full speed into a wall. His glasses flew off as he went tumbling round and round like a football rolling fast down a hill. He finally came to a stop and looked up to find Rex in mid-air about to pounce down upon him!

Arnold jumped at the last second and just barely got away, running off in any direction he could. But he was exhausted and dazed by the blow. He was also very dizzy having rolled down the hill so fast, and almost blind without his glasses.

Rex growled and barked with even greater anger as his jaws snapped at Arnold's tail not once, not twice, but three times! Arnold ran in a zigzag pattern, trying to confuse the dog and get away! It worked for a little while, but he was growing tired, and Rex was just getting started.

Rex gave out a great howl and leaped right onto Arnold's back and seized him in with his sharp teeth and lifted him high into the air. Arnold squirmed with intense fear, but thankfully the topside of an armadillo is the strong side and his thick skin of armor prevented Rex's jaws from digging in and getting a firm hold on him. Rex shook Arnold violently back and forth in his mouth, but ended up throwing him down another hill.

Arnold flipped around over and over again, shouting all the way until he finally came to a stop by hitting the bottom of an old tree stump. It was over, and he was doomed at last. He had no more energy, no more escape routes, and
nothing else to do but wait. And he didn't have to wait long.

In a flash, Rex appeared from the top of the hill and looked straight at him. He growled and let huge drips of foam flow down from his mouth, his teeth shining bright in the sunlight, and the hair on his back rose straight up in rage!

He leaned back onto his hind legs and leaped up into the air! He was about to pounce onto Arnold who closed his eyes and waited for the end to come. Suddenly, at the last possible moment, Arnold felt a swift wind sweep over top of him from behind. Then he heard a terrible crashing of bodies and growls, terrible yelps and thumps as two great bodies might make as they collided in midair above him, and fell over to the ground next to him.

Arnold opened his eyes, amazed to find he was still alive and could see two dogs fighting each other on the ground only a few feet away from him. He moved quickly away, back toward the woods to watch when he stumbled upon his glasses. He put them on and looked back at the fight. It was then that he realized just what had happened.

Just as Rex was about to land onto Arnold, Boomer had miraculously leapt out of the woods from behind him and collided with Rex. Now the two were battling it out on the ground, jaws thrashing, legs and claws flailing, and moans echoing all throughout the yard.

The two great hounds wrestled each other for what seemed like hours! Neither one giving up, and both biting and scratching each other! Arnold was very worried for his dear old friend, who never seemed to care much about being noble, or much about anything except sleep and bacon! He had grown to love his dear friend, but he was old, and he never thought of Boomer as being able to fight a dog before, especially not one as vicious and mean as Rex. They rolled their way into the woods where after a few minutes they all heard a terrible loud yelp of pain from one of the dogs. Then, everything suddenly became very still and silent.

Otto, Huck, and Rags all joined Arnold now as they watched the woods, waiting to see what had happened. Then, slowly, with a limp, came Boomer walking out of the woods. He was scratched and bleeding in several places, and his mouth also dripped with blood, but it was not his own blood.

The friends all cried with joy as Boomer walked out a hero, having saved Arnold's life.

"But I thought you didn't care?" Arnold asked of his friend, with tears in his eyes.

"So, I lied," Boomer said in his usual deep low voice, as if he was ready for a nice long nap. His wounds would heal and he even managed a little smile when he saw how touched Arnold was. Arnold remembered what the Duke had said about friends. But apparently the Duke never had friends like he did. Friends willing to sacrifice for each other – to stand by each other no matter what.

"But how did you know?" Arnold asked.

"All the noise from the kennel woke me from my nap!" Boomer snapped. "I figured you'd gotten yourself in some kind of mess!" They all laughed.

"I'll get as much bacon for you as I can!" Arnold answered, and gave the great hound a tremendous hug.

"Don't worry, sometimes you have to stand up for what's right." Boomer said.

Arnold knew exactly what he meant. He had chosen to give himself up so that Rags could survive and be with

Huck. He would not let someone else suffer when he could be there to do something about it, no matter how difficult it might be. Arnold thought about it and said to himself, "I guess that's what love means."

They gathered around the boat, where Arnold and Huck told the others of their adventure. It had been a very long day, and night was coming fast.

"I guess we better get going" Arnold said. "I wish I didn't have to say goodbye, but I don't know where Huck, Rags and I will end up. I guess it will be wherever this creek takes us."

The others all began to laugh!

"What's so funny?" Arnold asked.

"The creek! It goes in a large loop around the neighborhood! We're right on the other side of Canterbury Park!" Otto explained.

"Yup," Boomer added, "We should be home for supper."

So the gang all returned home to Ellen and Andy's house where they told them of their adventures. Ellen and Andy walked Huck back to his home where his mother had been waiting. She was panicked that he was lost somewhere, and hugged him for a very long time upon seeing him again. Rags barked with joy as well.

"But I want to keep my puppy, mom!" Huck cried. "Please don't send him away!"

"But honey, we just cannot keep a dog, I'm so sorry." His mother answered. At this news, Huck began to cry. It was he who made the sign when he had to leave Rags for the night, so no one knew who his owner was, and no one was looking for him.

"I have an idea!" Ellen said. "I'll bet Mrs. Dykwell would love a puppy! She lives alone and seems so sad. I'm sure she'll take Rags if we ask her! That way you can see and play with him every day, Huck!"

Huck loved the idea, and so did Rags. Ellen and Andy made their way quickly over to Mrs. Dykwell's house and returned with the news that she would be happy to take Rags. They all cheered and the next day, Huck, Ellen, and Andy all took Rags over to his new home, and Huck promised never to run away again.

Chapter 9

Arnoldwulf

Legends aren't born so much as they evolve. The memories of a fantastic event are buried for a year or two, until the stories grow hazy enough for them to become legends. Then, they become timeless, somewhat embellished, but always with just enough truth to survive. Such was the event which would eventually lead to the legend of Arnoldwulf! The bravest armadillo ever.

Arnold never saw himself as a legend. In fact, he had proven to be a somewhat clumsy and even reckless little armadillo. He had a tremendous heart and sought to do good things with it, and nothing gave him more joy than to help others in need. There were times when Ellen or Andy would have something go wrong and would be upset and crying. He would always be there to listen and to cheer them up by slipping down the slide, accidently hitting his head against something hard because he forgot his glasses, or just by telling a funny armadillo story which seemed so short and simple that the kids often laughed, just because.

But deep inside, Arnold felt like a bit of a failure. He had been rescued by his friends on many occasions and always seemed to be learning lessons from his mistakes. While learning from mistakes is one of the most important things you can ever do in life, Arnold felt like he wanted to do something on his own. So one day when a young little armadillo from a nearby neighborhood suddenly showed up, Arnold took it as his call to arms.

"Ahoy there!" a little voice called up into the Fort where Arnold had been resting on a crisp, cool, clean morning. It was New Year's Eve, a time for resolutions and new beginnings. And most of all, it was a time for fun. But Arnold wasn't expecting visitors.

"Who's there?" asked Arnold, not recognizing the voice.

"Tried and true, 'tis Tiny Todd from Troy to you!" Tiny Todd called. Tiny Todd was indeed a tiny armadillo, and spoke in alliteration, as was his habit. And he was tiny, not much larger than a chipmunk.

"Tried and true?" wondered Arnold, "What do you want?"

"To tell you a terrible, trembling tale with the hope that you'll happily help a helpless, but not hopeless, friend," Tiny Todd called back.

"Helpless? Hopeless? Happy?" Arnold said out loud as he yawned, still tired. "What are you talking about?" he asked.

"Wow! That's some slick and slippery super looking slide!" Tiny Todd stated. He was apparently easily distracted.

"The slide?" Arnold asked once more. "Oh, hey, let me slide down and we can talk." Arnold got a running start and took off down the slide at high speed! He was ready to fly off into the air when he noticed, to his dismay, Tiny Todd sitting naively right in the middle of it near the bottom.

"Look out!" Arnold called, but it was too late. Arnold was more than twice as large as tiny Todd and he rammed into him so hard it was like a baseball being struck by a huge bat! Tiny Todd when flying high into the air and came down on the other side of the yard, right into one of the metal trash cans! It was a slam dunk!

Arnold shook off the collision and ran over to check on Tiny Todd.

"Are you okay?" he asked, calling up to the top of the trash can. Then he began to hear some fumbling from within the can as if Tiny Todd was digging around inside, trying to figure out where he was and how to get out. Tiny Todd was fumbling in trash, which included wet papers, old coffee grounds, black and slimy banana peels, bits of rotting cabbage, and scraps of other vegetable and paper products. The smell was something fierce, but Tiny Todd had managed to knock the lid clean off, and now was scratching around the bottom of the can. It is natural for an armadillo to dig for safety when alarmed, but he was getting nowhere.

"Hello?" Arnold called again, this time he also tapped on the side of the metal can. The scratching and fumbling stopped, then started again. Suddenly, there was a loud thump from inside the can.

"Ouch!" an echoing little voice came from the can. "That wasn't good." Said Tiny Todd from deep under mounds of disgusting trash.

"Come on out of there!" Arnold, growing impatient, called out.

"Out? What a wonder to wonder where! Oh my, here is some stinky underwear!" Tiny Todd called from deep inside the disgusting trash can.

"Oh, enough is enough!" Arnold quickly moved over and tipped the entire can over on its side. Trash spilled out, but not Tiny Todd. He began to walk inside the can amongst the remaining trash like a hamster in an exercise wheel. The can slowly began to roll down toward the driveway onto the sidewalk, and from there down toward the street.

"Wait!" Arnold shouted, "Stop moving you dummy!" But Tiny Todd's little feet full of feverish energy kept moving faster and faster, and so did the can! It was loud, rattling and rolling along the edge of the road as a car whipped by almost hitting it straight on. Arnold knew he'd have to do something quick, or else watch this little armadillo be crushed by a passing car or truck.

Arnold ran ahead of the can toward Mrs. Dykwell's house where he noticed a large tree branch waiting to be picked up by the trash man. He rushed over pushed the branch in front of the rolling trash can just in time. The can came to a complete and sudden stop which jolted Tiny Todd who flipped around inside a couple of times before finally coming to rest himself. A long trail of trash was left behind the can leading all the way back to Ellen and Andy's backyard.

"Look what you've done!" an angry Arnold scolded as Tiny Todd wobbled out of the can, extremely dizzy and disoriented. But he quickly shook it off and smiled at his new, large armadillo friend.

"Holy heroics, my humongous helper!" said Tiny Todd, overcome with excitement.

"What?" said Arnold rather insulted, "What do you mean humongous?"

Tiny Todd looked as if he had been dipped in some of the most disgusting rotten garbage ever, and he smelled like it too. He was squinting his eyes trying to see clearly which is always hard for an armadillo without glasses like Arnold's.

"Wow! I've never known a giant armadillo with such supremely super sweet eyes!" said Tiny Todd, referring to Arnold's glasses.

"What?" said Arnold, then realizing what Tiny Todd was referring to he said, "Oh, these are just my..."

But Tiny Todd was too excited and interrupted saying, "You saved a fellow, foolish little friend, my friend! You're just the bravely bombastic battle ready barbarian we've been looking for!" Tiny Todd proclaimed.

"Bombastic, barbarian?" Arnold was growing annoyed and confused by Tiny Todd's words, especially because it was clear that Todd himself often didn't know what they meant.

"My neighboring neighborhood, is on its nerves!" Tiny Todd began to explain. "And all because of a vile villain who's violently vexing us!"

"Violent? Vexing? You're giving me a headache. What are you talking about?" Arnold asked.

"The ferociously fearful, fiery, fierce fox!" Tiny Todd answered.

"A fox?" Arnold asked, trying to understand.

"A ferociously fearful, fiery, fierce fox!" Todd reiterated, his little voice talking at high speed and full of excitement.

"A ferociously fearful, fiery, fierce fox is vexing you violently because he's a vile villain?" Arnold said in haste, and out of breath.

"Exactly!" Tiny Todd replied.

"And so if he's the vile villain who is vexing you violently, then you are..."

"Victims!" Tiny Todd interrupted.

"Victims. Right," Arnold took a deep breath and shook his head. "I feel like a victim right about now as well."

"So, you must come back with me!" tiny Todd said.

"To do what?" Arnold asked.

"I promised to bring back the biggest, boldest, baddest armadillo of any and all!" Tiny Todd paused and then said slowly and with emphasis, "Armadillowulf!"

"Well, I'm not Armadillowulf," Arnold said bluntly, "I'm Arnold, and I have work to do." And he began to walk away.

"Arnold!" Tiny Todd insisted and began to chase after him, "You have proven that you are the smartest, slickest, surrealist armadillo of the land! Why, if you're not already a legend you soon will be!"

"Legend?" Arnold stopped at the sound of that word.

"Oh yes, the most legendary legend that would linger in lore and the like!" Tiny Todd said in his squeaky, speedy little voice. "Why I know that with every little legend there's a tiny trip of truth! And if you won't come, why it will mean the end of the chickens, the eggs, the birds, the cats, and the other armadillos."

"There are other armadillos too?" Arnold asked.

"Yes, and all in danger of the gravely grotesque and growling Grumpy." Todd said.

"And this Grumpy is..." Arnold asked

"The vile villain who is vexing violently the..."

"Please stop talking already!" Arnold interrupted Tiny Todd, "I'll go if you just stop talking like that!"

"Like what? Wait! You'll go? You will? You will! Yeah! I knew the legend of the bold and bald, bad and brave, beautiful and bodacious Armadillowulf was true!" Tiny Todd began to jump up and down, and flip over and over down the sidewalk. The pair began walking down the sidewalk, past Huck's house and out past the boundary of the neighborhood.

"But my name is Arnold!" Arnold said to clarify.

"Arnoldwulf! Yes, indeed! The hero of our hopeful and happy homestead!" Tiny Todd said, still jumping around with excitement that he could not contain.

"Arnoldwulf?" Arnold asked.

"Of course!" Tiny Todd explained, "Only a wulf will be able to fight off the fiercely frightful, ferocious fox!"

"I think you mean a wolf, like the animal. I'm not a wolf, I'm an armadillo!" Arnold wanted to make sure Todd was aware of this obvious fact before he'd make any promises of success.

"Arnoldwulf, absolutely!" Tiny Todd said. "You're most certainly not a wolf, but you're wonderfully willing, and walking my way! I'm sure it will work out."

The more Arnold thought about it, the more appealing it became, however, thinking of himself as a hero in his own right – not needing help from his friends. It seemed clear enough to Arnold that Tiny Todd was making more out of this fox business than what it could possibly be. It was probably just some animal tossing around garbage cans, or even more likely just a little skunk or something which was scaring this little armadillo. But still, if he were to become a legend in the neighborhood, he'd return home a true hero. And besides, he mainly thought he'd be helping the little guy out. So they walked for the better part of the morning, all the way across a second neighborhood to Tiny Todd's house.

It didn't take long for word to spread that their "Hero" had arrived. Tiny Todd's little voice announced to everyone that "Arnoldwulf" had arrived to scare away Grumpy, the evil fox. Soon all sorts of animals around the rural household were lining the pathway toward the house, cheering and welcoming Arnold. The backyard was gigantic and had a small chicken coop off to the corner under a large oak tree. Just on the other side of the tree stood a very tall slide and play set. It was at least twice as tall as Ellen and Andy's Fort, where he lived. In fact, everything here seemed larger and grander. There was even a giant yard gnome the animals had named, 'Troy'. It must have stood four or five feet tall! "Imagine what Mrs. Widmer would do with something like that," Arnold thought.

With all the attention, Arnold began to wonder what he had gotten himself into. If everything here was grander, then wouldn't it stand to reason that so was this Grumpy more of a real danger than he first thought?

All the animals gathered around to meet "Arnoldwulf." There were the chickens, of course, who were very excited to see their new protector, a variety of shabby looking squirrels, a few rabbits, moles, and even a few chipmunks. There were also two small twin cats, and a puppy who reminded Arnold of Rags, but he was even younger. No wonder they felt scared and intimidated by this Grumpy, they were all small little animals living in a very large and dangerous world.

Arnold wasn't comfortable with all the praise and attention he was receiving. He wasn't sure he could even help, much less live up to their expectations of him. If this fox were real, and he was beginning to believe he was, then he'd have to come up with a good plan right away. He may have only one chance to scare off this Grumpy, so he thought he'd better get it right the first time.

"So, what's your perceptively potent and powerful plan, Arnoldwulf?" Tiny Todd shouted, just as Arnold was beginning to wonder that same thing.

"Um..." Arnold said, trying to find something to say. He replied slowly, and with much less energy, "Perceptively... potent... and powerful... plan. Uh..."

The crowd of animals were growing uneasy at Arnold's hesitation. Tiny Todd began to look worried. He had been laughed at because he was so small and always seemed to be making mistakes and blunders. Perhaps this great "Arnoldwulf" would be yet another of his failings.

Arnold caught a glimpse of Tiny Todd's worried face, and smiled. He knew what it was like to be laughed at and made fun of, and he wasn't going to let Tiny Todd down.

"Well, you see, I have these very special, powerful glasses which allow me to do some magical things!" Arnold began to explain.

"Ohhh!" the animals all exhaled with amazement.

"Yes! I can read human writing, and even talk with them! And so, I think I will have a look around to see what I can find that might help me to scare this Grumpy away once and for all!"

"Yeah!" the animals cheered wildly as Arnold began walking over to the house. Although he put on a brave front, he was actually very frightened that he would fail these poor creatures and possibly get himself killed. He was hoping he might be able to find a nice child, like Ellen or Andy, living at this house, and then he'd try to reason with them and get them to help. But no one was home. So, he began walking around the house to go back to the backyard area.

As he was passing by the garage, he noticed a large package containing several brightly colored items laying down on the floor inside by the back corner. He moved closer to read the label on the package. It said, "Fireworks!" Of course! It was New Year's Eve and everyone would be lighting fireworks at midnight to celebrate the start of a New Year! Arnold knew about fireworks from when Ellen and Andy lit them on the Fourth of July! Arnold remembered that he thought the fireworks were quite loud, and he remembered how some popped and banged so loudly that it scared all the animals and even some kids in the neighborhood. It was by remembering this that suddenly Arnold had a great idea!

"When does this Grumpy usually come by?" Arnold asked.

"Late afternoon or dusk. Just before it gets dark," answered the twin kittens together in perfect harmony.

"Great! That will give us enough time. Help me drag this package to the backyard," Arnold ordered.

The animals all helped Arnold drag the large plastic bag full of fireworks to the backyard, just outside the chicken coop. The kittens used their claws to open the bag up so Arnold could grab each fire work and read the label. By reading the label he could tell what each firework was supposed to do. He then placed them in certain places all around the play set and the chicken coop. The firework set also came with a line of extra fuse which allowed you to tie all the fireworks together and light them at the same time.

There was one which shot a ball of fire straight up into the sky along with a loud whistle! Arnold asked the animals to dig a hole so he could bury it leaving just the top exposed so that it would look like the ground itself was launching balls of fire! Then he found others which would twirl and fly through the air leaving a trail of fire and light blazing across the sky. He had those placed just outside the chicken coop on an angle which would make them fly straight at the intruder. Finally, they found many packs of bottle rockets. Each rocket was designed to fly up into the air and explode with a loud bang! Arnold found a long plastic tube which once made up part of the chicken coop fence. He asked Tiny Todd to help him, when the time came, by lighting the rockets and feeding them into one end of the tube. He would point the other end directly at Grumpy and shoot them at him.

They all got to work setting up the fireworks. He directed where to dig the holes, how to position the flying spinners, and where to place the tube for the rockets. He tied the extra fuse to the Balls of Fire, and the others, then laid out all of the bottle rockets in places where it would make it easy for Tiny Todd to get them lit and into the tube at a high rate of speed! All was going perfectly when it occurred to Arnold that he had thought of everything, except how to light them. By this time everyone was in place, and it was getting dark. Grumpy would be there soon, and Arnold had no way of lighting the fireworks! He didn't show it, but inside he started to panic!

Just then, Arnold heard the scratching sound of a lighter flicking behind him. He turned around to see a single large bright orange flame glowing steadily from a small red lighter.

"Is this something you might be needing?" a voice asked as she held the lighter.

Arnold could not believe his eyes! "Irene!" he said. They both smiled, and after a moment Arnold said calmly and cleverly, "I love you."

"I know," Irene answered and smiled. "Let's get to work."

As they waited for Grumpy, Irene had the chance to explain that she had followed Demetri, the armadillo she planned to marry, all the way out to this neighborhood. But it just didn't feel right to her. He had a wonderful den, tons of grubs and garnishes, but something was always missing. It was a bond and a feeling she couldn't put into words. She realized that she had loved Arnold all along, but couldn't bring herself to return to him. She was too embarrassed and ashamed to go back, and yet, here he was selflessly coming to the rescue of others. She had found the lighter some time ago, but Demetri scoffed at how stupid it was because it was something no armadillo would ever need or want. Well, none except "Arnoldwulf!"

"That is fantastic," Arnold said about the lighter, "and wonderful to hear!" he said about her feelings toward him.

"We'll have plenty of time to talk more later" Irene insisted, "For now we need to get this trap set before Grumpy arrives, which could be any moment now."

The two armadillos finished laying out the fuse and explained the plan to all the other animals. The chickens were particularly nervous since they would be in charge of getting Grumpy to come close enough for the fireworks to scare him. If the plan failed, he would likely kill them all out of anger. Everyone held their breath and waited for Grumpy; they didn't have to wait long.

Arnold took his position just of behind a small wood pile and prepared to light the fuse. Then the small gate which lead into the backyard was flung open and slammed loudly against the fence. A low but ominous snarl broke the silence and the chickens began to dance around, nervously pacing back and forth around the coop.

Grumpy approached, sniffed and said, "Who's been here? I smell someone new."

The chickens jumped around in fear and as two ran around in circles they actually ran straight into one another knocking each other down to the ground.

Grumpy began to walk slowly toward the chicken coop. He was a large, slim red fox with battle scars across his skin and face. He was worn and wild, and his eyes were like lightning bolts of determination and evil. He was almost on top of the Balls of Fire when Tiny Todd shouted from on top of the chicken coop.

"Fire away!"

Grumpy paused. But nothing happened. Nothing seemed to move and no sound was heard. Well, except the sound of a very frightened Tiny Todd swallowing a loud single gulp.

"What did you say?" groaned Grumpy, squinting his evil yellow eyes onto Tiny Todd.

"I... I mean... I said... well, what I meant to say... that is... I would set a fire?" Tiny Todd nervously mumbled.

Grumpy was in no mood for games and marched straight over toward the coop, ready to help himself to a meal. It was then he heard a flick sound from behind the coop. He looked around but didn't see anything. A moment later, right above his head, came twirls of bright red, green, and orange flames! An instant later, they flew off into the air all over the place and then dropped down onto the ground one by one like giant flaming snowflakes.

Grumpy began to dance around, trying to dodge the flying fireworks, and slowly began to move backward toward the buried Balls of Fire firework.

"A little closer," Whispered Arnold to no one, as he was standing alone behind the wood pile, having just returned from lighting the fuse to the other fireworks. "Come on, closer you stupid fox!" he whispered intensely to himself.

It seemed like forever, but slowly Grumpy moved back ward as he was trying hard to track the flying fireworks, and to figure out what was really going on. Then, suddenly, the fireworks stopped. They had burned out. Grumpy was

Grumpy

still there, and didn't look scared in the least.

As silence overtook the backyard, Arnold looked up over top of the wood pile and noticed that Grumpy had backed up to a point where he was standing directly over the top of the buried Balls of Fire! It couldn't have been more perfect! "Flick!" Arnold lite the fuse, and ran back toward the gate, out in the open, to make sure Grumpy stayed right there.

Grumpy heard him and turned around, away from the chicken coop, but directly toward Arnold with the fence gate behind him.

"Who are you?" Grumpy asked, in an evil yet puzzled tone of voice.

"I AM ARNOLDWULF!!!" Arnold screamed!

Just as Arnold screamed, a giant ball of fire erupted from right below Grumpy's belly! The hot flame was instantly followed by an amazing cascade of bright flames forming large balls of fire ripping toward the sky to the sound of a super loud whistle!

Irene lit the bottle rockets and placed them in the pipe as Tiny Todd aimed it, leaning up against the top of the chicken wire fence that surrounded the coop. The rockets shot off and hit Grumpy square in the side, exploding on impact! Then one landed right on his tail, lighting it on fire as it exploded and caused Grumpy to go absolutely crazy with fear!

Grumpy leaped higher than the top of the chicken coop he was so scared! He landed back down on the very same spot, just in time for another ball of fire to blast him in the jaw! He yelped like a scared little puppy, and began to run toward Arnold and to escape!

Arnold didn't know what to do when he saw a large flaming fox fleeing toward him. But Grumpy was in no mood to fight. He simply leaped over top of Arnold and over top the gate. None of the animals had ever seen anyone run away so fast! He was truly the most frightened fox ever!

The animals all began to celebrate by shouting, "Arnoldwulf! – Arnoldwulf! – Arnoldwulf!" Not since Dorothy dropped a house onto the Wicked Witch of the East in the Wizard of Oz had there been so much joy! The gravely grotesque and growling Grumpy was gone for good and they now had a hero to thank!

The animal's cheers were followed by their own version of music and dancing, late into the night. They shot off the remaining fireworks to celebrate what promised to be a wonderful new year, free of terror – free of Grumpy the fox! And Arnold and Irene spent time planning their future together. The celebration lasted well into the night and into the next morning before they finally all made it to their first restful sleep in ages.

All was quiet when Arnold woke the next morning, still a recovering from the drama and celebration. But something was terribly wrong. As soon as he woke he heard the chickens scatter and clucking in panic. The cats, squirrels, birds and other creatures went scattering for cover amongst the bushes and shrubs. Arnold knew something was wrong.

As he peeked around the edge of the wood pile into the backyard, he understood why everyone was scared. There stood a large red fox with sheets of long gray hair its sides. It stood there at attention, and was almost twice the size of Grumpy. And this fox was angry.

Arnold rubbed his eyes, hoping he was still dreaming, but this was not a dream. The fox's paw dug into the dirt where the Balls of Fire had been buried, and within a second, the firework was exposed and lifted out of the ground. There would be no fooling *this* fox.

"Where is this thing called, Arnoldwulf?" the fox calmly, but sternly, asked the animals. "I know you're all hiding. Someone had better answer me."

Suddenly, Tiny Todd snuck up next to Arnold and whispered to him, "It's grumpy Grumpy's insanely morose and morbid mother! She's come to kill us all!" his worried little voice trailed off into a faint whisper. Arnold swallowed hard, he was very frightened.

Grumpy's mother walked slowly toward the chicken coop, and right into the chicken wire fence, gently pushing it aside, and straight on into the coop itself. She returned with an egg inside her mouth and walked back out in front of the swing set.

She looked around for a moment, then snapped her jaws shut, smashing the egg. Still dripping from her mouth she spit out the remaining shell fragments and said, "This is just the beginning until I find this Arnoldwulf." It was a threat she intended to keep.

Arnold tried to think of what to do. He could go out and sacrifice himself, but that would not only destroy the legend he'd created, but also endanger his new friends who would have to endure Grumpy's mother's wrath. The only choice was to fight. But how can an armadillo fight a fox and win?

"What are you going to do?" asked Tiny Todd, so scared that he stopped talking in alliteration.

Arnold looked down at Tiny Todd, and then the idea came to him!

"Yes!" Arnold said to Tiny Todd. "Thank you Tiny Todd! I know exactly what I'm going to do. It may not work, but I'm going to give it everything I have!" Arnold said, then he took off along the front of the wood pile toward the swing set.

"Huh?" Tiny Todd said as Arnold left. Then he took up a position on the top of the woodpile in order to see what Arnold was planning.

Arnold quickly, but quietly, scampered up the tall ladder of the giant slide. The slide was easily twice as tall and fast as his own back at Ellen and Andy's house. He reached the very top and looked down. It was higher up than he'd ever been before, and down below, right in front of the slide, was Grumpy's mother. She was looking down toward the ground, walking around in a little circle, and growling.

Arnold knew he'd have only one chance, but he remembered how back home he struck Tiny Todd as he slide and launched him into a garbage can. Perhaps he could do the same with Grumpy's mother, or at least scare her into leaving. If he failed, he knew he would be a dreadfully dead armadillo; but he had no other choice. He wouldn't just leave his new friends and run away from danger. He took a deep breath, adjusted his glasses, and then launched himself down the slide as fast and as hard as he could.

As Arnold picked up speed, Grumpy's mother was still pacing below. Arnold was sliding at a super high speed down the slide and he flew off the end like a bullet! His nose straight out, his body appeared more like an armored missile – or more accurately, an armadillo missile! The slide propelled him into the air and straight toward Grumpy's unsuspecting mother.

At the very last moment, Arnold yelled at the top of his lungs, "Ahhh!!!" Before Grumpy's mother could turn around to see him, he struck her in the side so hard that he knocked her over and rolled her three times before she finally came to rest. She felt as if someone had kicked her in the stomach, she was gasping for air, and almost blacked out. She had hit her head on a rock which made everything seem like a spinning, dizzy blur.

Arnold had come to rest pretty much where he had struck her, but he quickly noticed that he was very disoriented, and had lost his glasses. Several feet away, Grumpy's mother was trying to get back onto her feet. She didn't realize that with the collision, somehow Arnold's glasses ended up on her face!

A fox typically has fantastic eyesight, so Arnold glasses actually made her eyes much worse. It was like putting on a pair of glasses that didn't belong to you. She couldn't see much of anything, and what she did see was greatly out of proportion. When she finally looked over toward Arnold, the glasses made him look like a gigantic armadillo over ten feet tall!

Arnold took to his feet, able only to see a blur in front of him which he knew was Grumpy's mother. Without thinking, acting more on instinct than anything else, he decided to charge at her! He began flailing his arms up and down and ran toward her with an insane scream! "Ahhh!!!!" he shouted, his voice booming with all his energy!

Thanks to the glasses, Grumpy's mother thought she saw a giant, ten foot tall, vicious and crazy armadillo rushing at her! For the first time in her life, she was truly frightened beyond her wits! In her mind, she had just been punched by this giant armadillo, this Arnoldwulf! Now, he was running toward her with giant arms and teeth! She knew she would be killed if she stayed! So she quickly took off and ran as fast as she could, never to return.

In her haste, as she tore off for the gate to escape, she flung Arnold's glasses off into the air and they landed right onto Arnold's face. He immediately stopped running and screaming as he realized the she had disappeared. A wonderful feeling of accomplishment settled into his stomach, as he realized that he was a true hero and had saved the day. Neither Grumpy, nor his mother, were ever heard from again.

The animals once again cheered, "Arnoldwulf! – Arnoldwulf – Arnoldwulf!" and invited him to stay and live with them. But Arnold and Irene both agreed that they would be happier at home with Ellen and Andy. They said goodbye, and began a long slow walk home together. It

186

certainly looked as though it would be the happiest of New Years!

Chapter 10

The Face the Launched
A Thousand Armadillos

It had been an amazing spring! Arnold and Irene had grown happier than ever and were living in the Fort atop the play set in Ellen and Andy's backyard. The crisp winter winds had given way to warmer spring breezes, and there were fantastic smells of rotting wood, fresh grubs and worms, and the occasional strip of bacon! Tiny Todd had become used to making several trips back and forth to visit Arnold, and had gotten to know Ellen, Andy, Otto, Henry, and Boomer quite well.

The friends would play together all the time, including Tiny Todd's favorite game, Hide and Seek. Upon occasion, this game would lead him into Mrs. Widmer's backyard, for Tiny Todd was small enough to fit through a small opening in the bottom of the fence. He'd always win when he hid there because no one else dared to enter her yard for fear of a swift swat from her broom. And while Tiny Todd had been lucky so far, everyone warned him not to trespass in her garden. Arnold and Irene told him how they had barely escaped Mrs. Widmer with their lives! But Tiny Todd didn't think much about it. After all, it was such a beautiful and peaceful place.

Mrs. Widmer was out regularly tending to her backyard garden with fresh woodchips, flowers, and plants, pulling every little weed, and delicately placing every garden gnome and decoration. There were several bird houses and feeders, the fountain was flowing like a peaceful little stream, the windmill turned gently in the warm breeze, and she had recently completed a wonderful gazebo in which she and her dog Penni would sit and bask in the aroma of her garden and the fresh spring air. It was topped off with a small statue of a golden apple – representing something divine, and peaceful. The golden apple was legendary for being a gift from the Greek gods to the fairest of them all. In Arnold's mind, that certainly meant Irene, not Mrs. Widmer. Still, it was a time of peace and happiness for all; but that peace was about to broken.

Mrs. Widmer had spent a considerable amount of time and money to spruce up and repair her backyard sanctuary. She always kept a sharp eye on possible invaders, and had begun to notice tiny holes along the back side of her garden. The kind of holes only an armadillo could make. She sent Penni out on patrol to keep an eye out for any intruders, but Penni was already scared of her own shadow, and tended to run away from a large insect if Mrs. Widmer wasn't by her side. Nevertheless, one day she stumbled across Tiny Todd who was playing Hide and Seek and hiding just behind a small lilac bush. It was a complete accident that she found him, and she almost ran right into him! Both Penni and Tiny Todd jumped from surprise and Penni let out a very loud and distinctive bark!

Immediately, Mrs. Widmer turned toward the fence and Penni. Her eyes narrowed and her nose curled. She grabbed her broom and made her way swiftly toward the edge of the garden. Tiny Todd was cornered by Penni who was not actually acting brave so much as she was simply scared stiff and unable to move a muscle. It was probably the only time Tiny Todd ever intimidated anyone – but he was even more frightened, for he knew Mrs. Widmer was near. Mrs. Widmer approached from behind her and in one fell swoop her broom swung down and smacked Tiny Todd so hard that he flew up into the air and over the fence into Ellen and Andy's yard, landing right in front of Henry, Mr. Baker's cat.

"Hey! I didn't know armadillos could fly!" Henry smiled and joked.

Still dazed and rubbing his head, Tiny Todd said angrily, "We can't! That hideously horrible old hag flung me over the fence!"

"We've told you not to go over there," Henry replied.

"I know, I know, but it is so nice over there. And in any case, I wasn't doing anything wrong!" Tiny Todd said.

"You don't have to be doing something wrong – going there at all is wrong." Henry added. "Come on, let's find the others and start a new game."

The friends all gathered and began to play a new game. Thinking about it, Tiny Todd decided that the best hiding place for this round would be right back in Mrs. Widmer's garden! No one would ever go look for him there because he'd be a fool to try to hide there again after what just happened. Also, he believed Penni and Mrs. Widmer would probably not be looking for him again and he would stay near the fence so he could run back quickly enough if he needed to. So, as Irene was counting down from 19, preparing to go search for everyone, he took off for Mrs. Widmer's.

"Ready or not, here I come!" Irene announced.

Arnold, Henry, and Otto were all hiding as Irene slid down the slide and proceeded to follow her nose in search of them. Her nose was crafty and sharp, but the animals had tracked in so many directions recently that she

Mrs. Widmer's Beautiful Garden

couldn't really distinguish between who was who and
where they had been. But there seemed a fresh trail of lilac
smell trailing off toward Mrs. Widmer's yard – a smell Tiny
Todd had picked up while he was over there last time. She
suspected that Tiny Todd was back there again and
decided to follow the scent. If she was right, she was
prepared to teach him a lesson about going where he

shouldn't. They may not really like Mrs. Widmer, but they all had decided to respect her privacy and to leave her garden alone – for their own safety.

Sure enough, the lilac scent led directly to the small crack in the fence. Irene didn't know if she'd be small enough to squeeze through, but she managed to do so after some effort. She flung herself into the garden – a place she hadn't been since Arnold took her there months ago. It was beautiful. She took a moment to stare up at the flowers and trees. Being spring time, she couldn't resist taking a long deep breath of the most pleasant smells a flower can produce.

The moment ended quickly when she saw Tiny Todd dive off into a small shrub just down the path. She walked over to find him, turned and stood on her two hind legs and was ready to pounce onto him in order to scare him. But just as she stood, a large presence appeared from just behind her, casting a large shadow over her and Tiny Todd who looked up in fear!

"SLAM!!!" a box fell down upon Irene so fast she had no chance to react. Tiny Todd took off for the fence and escaped to the sound of Penni barking in the distance.

"Arnold, Arnold!" he shouted in panic as he raced up the ladder and into the Fort.

Arnold quickly came out from his hiding place and rushed up to meet Tiny Todd. Otto and Henry soon followed.

"A giant trapped her! I ran, but she's gone! Oh my, she's gone!" Tiny Todd cried and whined inconsolably. "It's all my fault! I knew I shouldn't have gone back there!"

"Calm down!" Otto ordered, "Let's see what this is all about first." Otto always kept his cool.

They looked out from atop the play set to see Mrs. Widmer carrying a wooden crate back to her house, toward the garage. As her garden began to obstruct the view, Otto jumped up to the top of the canopy and continued to track her.

"She took Irene into the garage," Otto announced. "She's a prisoner."

Arnold just stared – speechless. He was stunned at what had just happened, and his friends were quickly growing concerned. Otto began to think about a plan to rescue Irene, but given Mrs. Widmer's new attention to securing her property all he could come up with amounted to nothing more than hope, and for Arnold that wasn't enough. He stayed quiet while his friends were talking about what to do. After a long while, he broke his silence with a tone of voice that meant business. "Go get Troy," he said.

"Who's Troy?" asked Henry.

"You mean, big Troy?" asked Tiny Todd, who knew that Arnold was referring to the giant garden gnome back in his neighborhood.

"Yes. And also..." Arnold leaned over and whispered into Tiny Todd's ear some special instructions.

"You want me to do what?" Tiny Todd asked in amazement.

"Shh! I mean it!" Arnold scolded, then began to whisper more. Finally, Tiny Todd stared at Arnold for a long moment, took a deep breath, and nodded his head in agreement. Then he took off down the slide and toward his home neighborhood in haste.

"What's going on?" asked Henry.

"I have to go," Arnold said, and then turning to his friends he added, "If I don't come back, please say goodbye to Ellen and Andy for me."

Henry and Otto were stunned as Arnold then took off down the slide and ran off. He wasn't heard from the rest of the day.

That night would be a very busy one for Arnold and his friends. In just a few hours he had spread the word among all the armadillos he knew that his love, the beautiful Irene, had been kidnapped, and that he needed their help to rescue her. Arnold went home and found his old friends Willie and Mitch the armadillos, which along with him began to spread the word of what had happened. Every armadillo who heard began to tell others, and soon there were armadillos from neighboring neighborhoods and far off places coming out to join in what simply became a giant crusade.

Arnold was coordinating the armadillos like a general, and the plan being worked out to rescue Irene was complicated for them to understand. But with the wisdom he had gained by reading books thanks to his magical glasses, he would manage and lead them – and with their numbers, they would succeed! They would rescue Irene and deal with Mrs. Widmer once and for all.

They met late that night just down the road from Mrs. Widmer's house. Tiny Todd had brought with him the giant garden gnome they had named Troy, along with at least a dozen of his closest armadillo friends.

"Okay, here's what we're going to do," Arnold explained to Tiny Todd and his friends. "I want you all to climb inside with Willie and Mitch. You will stay there and very quiet until morning when Mrs. Widmer will see Troy standing at her front door. She will think it's a gift being delivered, a surprise. And boy it's going to be a surprise alright! She will naturally take it inside her garden. You will wait for night to come, and then sneak out of the gnome and open the gate so that the rest of us can come inside. Once we surround the house, we will force Mrs. Widmer to give us Irene!"

The others cheered at the plan like a giant anxious crowd of soldiers about to invade and attack the enemy. Tiny Todd led the way into the gnome through a small hatch in its tummy, being the smallest of them all. After about twelve other armadillos squeezed into the gnome, Tiny Todd was being squished up against the very top. The last ones in were Mitch and Willie, who would open the door and sneak out when the time was right. Once inside, the others began to push the giant garden gnome down the road toward Mrs. Widmer's house.

"Oh no!" Tiny Todd whispered.

"What is it?" The other armadillos beneath him asked, somewhat annoyed.

"I was just thinking... Oh, how I wish I had gone to the bathroom," Tiny Todd explained.

"You had better hold it!" Willie announced, and all the other armadillos, being underneath Tiny Todd, agreed.

"Yeah, I'll try. Just don't bump!" said Tiny Todd.

Just then they hit a large bump! All the other armadillos looked up toward Tiny Todd resting on top, and waited for any signs of dripping.

"Holding!" Tiny Todd announced, half smiling out of happiness and half out of fear that he wouldn't be able to hold it much longer. For now at least, everyone else was relieved and dry.

It is said that gnomes represent guardians of treasure and often contain hidden fortunes and good luck charms. Mrs. Widmer certainly believed in the good fortune associated with gnomes, but she was in for a big surprise at what this gnome contained. The gnome finally arrived at Mrs. Widmer's just before sunrise. The others took their places among the trees and bushes around her house. By mid-morning, Mrs. Widmer opened her front door and looked around, and then at the giant gnome. She inspected it carefully, and then wheeled it toward the side yard, just as Arnold expected. She locked the gate behind her. The smile on her face showed that she was delighted with her wonderful gift.

She placed it right at the center of her garden, where three other little pathways came together. She stepped back from it and looked at it admiringly.

"It is almost four feet tall and a wonderful centerpiece to the garden," she thought.

But inside, things were less settled. The armadillos were growing cramped, and Tiny Todd had another feeling going on inside. He wasn't nervous, but it was a kind of pressure that had built up in his gut. He was struggling to hold it throughout the whole trip, but he just couldn't any longer. Without warning to the others, Tiny Todd suddenly ripped a gigantic fart!

The hideous smell quickly sank down among the other armadillos who began to move about in a small panic, wheezing and gasping for fresh air like bees cramped up into a bee hive stirring with activity! Tiny Todd was so distraught that he ripped a second monster fart, far more pungent than the first! The others now began to move much more violently and began pleading to be let out of what they now called, the gas chamber!

Outside, Mrs. Widmer noticed what sounded like a large hungry stomach churning! Then the gnome began to rock slowly back and forth. She moved in closer to it to see what could possibly be wrong. The rocking grew more intense, and the noise louder and louder until it seemed as if the gnome was coming to life! Her eyes widened as she got close enough to touch the gnome's tummy – then all of the sudden the hatch flew open and Mitch literally flew out banging head to head with Mrs. Widmer, knocking her down to the ground on her backside.

Willie and the others quickly followed as a flow of armadillos began to pour out of the stinky gnome as fast as they could. They rolled out, tumbling on top of one another. It seemed impossible to have squeezed so many armadillos inside such a statue. Armadillos began to pile up on top of Mrs. Widmer's legs and stomach until finally the last armadillo, Tiny Todd, rolled down the mountain of armadillos, flew out of the gnome and landed right on Mrs. Widmer's chest.

"Ahh!!!" Mrs. Widmer finally screamed in pure fright!

"Ahh!!!" Tiny Todd screamed back at her, face to face! They continued screaming at each other in terror when Tiny Todd lost control and began to pee all over Mrs. Widmer!

The screaming only got worse as the armadillos scattered in all directions, and the chaos began.

"Mitch, we have to get to the gate!" Willie shouted. Both he and Mitch made their way quickly toward the gate. Mitch climbed up onto Willie's back and managed to reach the latch and open it. In no time at all, a sea of armadillos began to pour into Mrs. Widmer's backyard garden. Mrs. Widmer screamed like she had never screamed before. It was sheer panic and fright as if her life was literally on the line. Still covered in dirt and pee, she ran into the house as fast as she could, slamming the door behind her. Almost immediately, armadillos began to nip at her heels through the little pet door Penni would use to go in and out of the house. Mrs. Widmer bent down and locked the pet door, but she knew it would only be a matter of time before the armadillos would break through.

By this time, all the commotion had gotten the attention of Arnold's friends who had all made their way to the top of the fort in order to see what was happening. The sight was something they would never have believed if they hadn't seen it for themselves. There they were, Otto,

Henry, Rags, Huck, Ellen, Andy, and even Boomer, all watching the chaos unfold with their jaws dropped in disbelief. All they could do was watch in total shock and disbelief as Mrs. Widmer's backyard paradise was ripped to shreds by what must have been at least one thousand armadillos.

The armadillos struck Mrs. Widmer's Achilles heel! They were everywhere! Armadillos were plowing up rare plants and tossing around little garden gnomes like footballs. Dirt was being flung through the air in all directions, the bird bath and fountains were being toppled leaving water shooting through the air. The sprinkler system was struck and pierced which instantly began flooding the entire backyard, slowly turning it into a gigantic mud bath! Lawn chairs were smashed and tossed around, and Mrs. Widmer's fantastic wooden gazebo soon looked like the leaning tower of Pisa as it began to snap under the pressure of burrowing armadillos from all directions. The potted plants were tipped and broken, the pathways were blended into a giant mesh of garden foliage and woodchips.

Mrs. Widmer's precious little dog Penni could be heard barking at the top of her little lungs from inside Mrs. Widmer's two story house. The kids spotted her looking out from a window upstairs. She looked scared to death as armadillos began streaming into the house through the pet door below. But a fantastic cheer sprang up from the armadillos in the yard when suddenly they finally managed to open the main door from the backyard into the house. The armadillos rushed inside, climbing over top one another in order to get in first. They seemed possessed, as if they were on a grand crusade to rid the neighborhood of an evil enemy and rescue one of their own who had been taken and so cruelly treated.

Once inside Mrs. Widmer's house, the armadillos completely lost control of themselves and went on a vicious rampage of destruction. Her beautiful, crisp mint green carpet was quickly soiled with mud and the revolting odor of hundreds of armadillos scattering in all directions, their trampling feet sounding like running horses! The carpet was soon torn up and armadillos began to dig and burrow under it all around the house. The cushions of the chairs and couches were torn open leaving a billowing cloud of white stuffing and feathers floating about the rooms. Knick knacks and books were thrown from the ever so neat and tidy bookshelves onto the floor with the sound of breaking glass! Armadillos even got into the bathrooms and began running around the entire house trailing toilet paper behind them everywhere! Tiny Todd found the first floor toilet to be just his size and hopped in to take a quick bath! Another armadillo, Mitch, flushed the toilet sending Tiny Todd slushing around, spinning him around in a circle!

"Weee!!!" Tiny Todd shouted! "It's a whirlpool!" his excitement couldn't be contained. "Do it again, Mitch! Flush it again!"

Mitch flushed again, but this time Tiny Todd's bottom got caught in the toilet which was sucking him downward into the pipe.

"Oh no! I'm stuck! Help!" Tiny Todd shouted. But by this time, Mitch had moved on to continue exploring and destroying Mrs. Widmer's house. Tiny Todd remained there shouting for help when another armadillo managed to kick the toilet lid down over him, leaving him stuck there in the dark, screaming for help amongst the chaos.

Meanwhile, the kitchen was fairing no better. Armadillos were stacked two to three layers deep on the floor, and had propped open the refrigerator. Sounds of pots and pans banging, glasses breaking, and water running seemed louder than an airplane. Food was being quickly thrown out with bottles of soda being shaken and suddenly opened, shooting foam across the kitchen like a rocket. The armadillos began sliding across the smooth floor on sticks of butter like skis and turning the entire kitchen into a massive Slip and Slide. On top of the refrigerator, another set of armadillos had broken into a huge bag of Cheetos and were now covered in the tasty bright orange residue. Others had found the storage of Tang, the powdered drink mix, which was then dropped down onto the crowd of armadillos on the floor leaving a light orange mist glowing in the morning sunlight which was now beginning to stream into the house.

"Oh, I like Tang!" one armadillo was overheard saying. They were climbing, jumping, rolling, crashing, singing, spitting, sneezing, farting, pooping, peeing, and dancing all over the entire house.

Hundreds upon hundreds of armadillos were still pouring in through the back door as Mrs. Widmer escaped up the stairs, into her bedroom where she closed and locked the door.

By now, armadillos were moving through the kitchen like a car moves through a car wash, except here they were being doused with broken eggs, corn meal, flour, milk, leftover spaghetti sauce, soda pop, vegetables, blueberries, strawberries, Cheerios and Grape Nuts flying everywhere with ketchup, barbeque, and ranch sauces pouring onto the sea of armadillos. Then, as one armadillo on the kitchen floor looked up, he saw a giant watermelon being pushed off of the counter and onto the floor. It exploded amongst the crowd like a fantastic firework in the sky! Watermelon was literally everywhere and the armadillos cheered eating and spitting seeds like little bullets at one another. The entire kitchen looked as if it were a giant mixing bowl of armadillos and gooey, sticky, yet tasty food being mixed and tossed. The kitchen chaos spread throughout the home as peanut butter and jelly plastered armadillos began to run in and out of the kitchen seeking new things to destroy. Mrs. Widmer's precious antique silver cutlery was discovered. Piece by piece were somehow thrown so hard across the room that forks and knives were jammed into the wall as cheers went up with every new successful throw.

Mrs. Widmer's antique hutch, all neatly arranged with fine china plates and knickknacks, began to rock slowly as mounds of armadillos rushed by it like a raging river. Soon the doors and drawers were opened and armadillos began climbing up and tossing cloth place settings and holiday decorations out into the mob below. Then, the top of the hutch began to rock and sway. The wine glasses and other crystal began to jingle. Eventually, the armadillos pushed and prodded the entire top of the hutch until it tipped over, smashing all the glass into the floor below in a gigantic crash! Don't worry, miraculously no armadillos were hurt during the telling of this story.

Eating a Cheeto!

In the laundry room, the washing machine had become a hot tub with a few armadillos being stirred around and around with bubbles overflowing. The entire box of soap had been spilled into the machine which kept filling with water as the armadillos splashed and spilled it all over the floor below. Soon suds were everywhere, filling the entire room from floor to ceiling. The suds grew and began to spread out into the hallway and into the kitchen and living room. The floors became super slick slides with armadillos running, falling, tripping, slipping, and sliding in every direction. They bumped, jumped, and flew into one another, all shouting with joy.

Anywhere and everywhere Mrs. Widmer's home was in a terrible frenzy! And now, that frenzy began to head up the stairs toward her bedroom.

"What are we going to do?" Andy asked

"I'm not sure there's anything we CAN do," replied Ellen. "I've never seen anything like this!"

From the Fort the scene looked like a bomb had gone off in Mrs. Widmer's garden. It now appeared to be a giant mud hole strewn with torn plants and shrubs, lawn furniture, and what was left of the windmill and gazebo. There were still some armadillos swimming around and sliding across the backyard in the mud as they gobbled up all kinds of worms and grubs that had been dislodged from their underground homes. They could only imagine what was going on inside.

Just then, Mrs. Widmer opened her bedroom window and began to scream, "Help!" She was holding Penni out over the yard. It looked like she was going to drop her in order to save her from the armadillo army that was beating on her door. But she wouldn't survive a fall from the second story window and Penni looked incredibly frightened.

"Let's go!" Andy shouted. Instantly, Ellen and Andy took off toward Mrs. Widmer's backyard in order to help and catch Penni. Both of them slipped many times on the muddy garden, and began laughing at how dirty and disgusting they were getting. They soon positioned themselves below Mrs. Widmer's window and then she dropped Penni. Ellen and Andy managed to catch her, and aside from getting some mud on her, Penni was just fine. They took her back to the Fort where she finally met Otto, Henry, Rags, and Boomer who quickly began to console and care for her.

Inside Mrs. Widmer's home, the upstairs was now being trashed by the rampaging armadillos. The guest rooms were tossed with bed sheets, towels, dresses, and shoes were flying everywhere. Several armadillos discovered how to use pieces of clothing to slide down the stairs – bumping and tumbling, doing summersaults all the way down. Eventually, over twenty armadillos piled onto a silk bed sheet and slide down the stairs with super speed. They slide onto the slippery soap bubbled hallway, and straight on toward the back door which led out to the muddy backyard. They blew through the doorway like a rocket and landed half way into the backyard, splashing mud in all directions! The armadillos all shouted with joy.

"Let's do that again!" they shouted, and began to pile back into the house. Ellen, Andy, and the other friends could do nothing but look on in shock, their mouths hanging open with Penni looking very worried.

After what seemed like hours, finally, the armadillo army slowly began to break up and leave Mrs. Widmer's house and yard. They were going home now, exhausted from the largest armadillo party they ever imagined. Mrs. Widmer managed to survive inside her bedroom, the sole survivor of what would go down in neighborhood history as the great Armadillo war. In time, many would doubt such a thing could have actually happened, but for those who were there and saw it, they would never forget what a thousand armadillos were capable of doing.

While all the armadillos were busy rampaging poor Mrs. Widmer's home, Arnold had snuck around to the front of the house and into garage which had been left open the whole time. He walked in and quickly found the box in which Irene had been captured. He managed to tip it over far enough to help Irene escape. They stood out front to watch the rest of the armadillos as they left for home, and then they decided to join them. It was not an easy decision to make, because Arnold truly loved his new friends, especially Ellen and Andy who had taught him so much and had shown him that the world around him was so much more than only what an armadillo could see and smell. It was a world of great beauty, sadness, and everything in between. The world around him seemed almost too much for him to handle, and he realized that his true happiness would be found by spending his life as armadillo's should – and with the love of his life.

He didn't know how to say goodbye to Ellen and Andy. So, remembering a story he had heard long ago, he wrote a little note for them. That night, after everyone had gone to bed, Arnold took off his glasses and left them and his note on Ellen and Andy's doorstep. Then, he and Irene left to join their fellow armadillos to live an armadillo's life.

The following morning, the friends gathered together in Ellen and Andy's Fort. They realized Arnold was missing, and had probably gone off with the other armadillos. They remembered their friend and were sad that he would no longer be there. From the house Ellen and Andy's father called for them to get ready for school. Life was already getting back to normal for everyone.

As they left the Fort, Ellen heard a small little sound coming from the bushes. Otto heard it too and quickly slide down the slide in order to investigate.

"What is that?" Andy asked.

"I don't know. Sounds like another kitty," Ellen answered.

Otto moved steadily toward the sound, moving faster and faster the closer he got. As he pushed through the bushes, he suddenly stopped in awe. Unbelievably, sitting there before him was a lonely, lost little kitten.

"Gisele!" Otto cried; she had returned to him at last. He had lost her months before, but now they were together. Ellen and Andy's Dad agreed to let Gisele stay with them, and their fairy tale finally had a happy ending. They lived a happy, playful life with each other, it was is if they were meant to be together. Sometimes fate has a funny way of working out in the long run.

Gisele

Huck took Rags back home with him, and they continued to visit often. Tiny Todd returned home to his neighborhood, telling phenomenal, frantically fantastic stories of the great Armadillo war to his friends. Henry and Boomer continued to live with Mr. Baker, enjoying a fairly quiet life with the occasional strip of crisp bacon that Andy would sneak over as often as he could.

The morning after the great Armadillo war, Mrs. Widmer was seen placing a "For Sale" sign in her front yard. It was the last anyone ever heard from her as she moved far away from Arnold the Armadillo.

Ellen and Andy missed their friend Arnold, but spoke of him often and laughed at his crazy adventures. They had found his glasses and kept them on their bookshelf next to a copy of this very book. Along with it was the note from Arnold which read:

Dear Ellen and Andy,
Remember, when the going gets rough
Be patient and true – that will be enough.
For all good things come to those who will wait
And learn to embrace the strange twists of fate.

Your dearest friend,

Arnold, the Armadillo

Epilogue

Behind the Scenes of
Arnold the Armadillo

Under the Garden Wall

One spring day a few years ago a family of four armadillos playfully made their way through our backyard. They seemed oblivious to my presence behind the den window as they were busy sniffing, digging, and rolling around in the dirt. I shouted for my kids, Ellen and Andy, to come watch them as they made their way right up next to the window. We laughed and admired the armadillos as cute and happy-go-lucky.

A year or so later, I was inspired by that memory to write a short story about an armadillo befriended by my kids. Thus, the first chapter was finished and I left it for over a year before picking it back up with a new idea – to send Arnold the Armadillo on a series of adventures that mirrored those of famous works of literature. Writing this book over the last several months has been a labor of love as Arnold has given me the opportunity to bond and remain close to my kids. I would write a chapter, then have them proof-read and give me feedback. Ellen was in charge of producing the illustrations, and Andy was in charge of story ideas and collaboration. I am blessed to know, and be so inspired by these two voracious readers whose contributions to Arnold's character have been significant. I love you both more than you could ever know. This book is for you, Ellen and Andy.

The concept of writing more adventures for Arnold came about when I realized that I was clueless when it came to developing a story out of thin air. So, by adapting Arnold's adventures from famous works of literature I discovered the working outline I needed. I thought it would also provide a creative way of introducing kids to these famous works of literature and their authors. I enjoyed re-reading many of them in order to find suitable adaptation points. Certainly these chapters are not tied too closely to the originals, but the connections are not hard to identify.

The Windmills are Weakening

The first literary connection seemed like a wonderful fit – Don Quixote (1605) by Miguel de Cervantes. This was the perfect spring board to introducing Arnold to his surroundings and to the reader as a character with a wonderful heart and soul. Since armadillo's cannot see well, if Arnold forgot his new glasses and had recently been told of knights and chivalry, he might start acting in a similar fashion to Don Quixote. I continued to develop the antagonist around Mrs. Widmer's character whose world could only be disturbed by outsiders, never improved.

The Canterbury Park Tales

The second connection was to the Canterbury Tales by Geoffrey Chaucer. The concept is similar, making a journey to a far off place and telling stories to pass the time. The two tales told were adapted from the Pardoner's Tale, and a couple of others. The most challenging portion of the book to write were the tales themselves which mimic Chaucer by using iambic pentameter. The stories were simple enough and held true to the moral message in Chaucer's originals while keeping a respectful distance from much of his more raw sensibilities.

The Hound of the Bakers

The third connection was to Sir Authur Conan Doyle's Sherlock Holmes. It was here that the characters began to develop more into their own. In this case the story was focused around Otto, who had been introduced in the prior chapter. Otto was named after the cat which appeared on the short-lived television show called, Bob – starring Bob Newhart. Otto was a very intelligent and mischievous cat on that show, so I felt that he'd be perfect to take on the role of Holmes. We had already introduced a hound, Boomer, and Arnold would be a great Watson. It just all seemed to fit. As much as I'd like to take credit for planning the entire book ahead of time, it was actually written in the order that the chapters appear with minimal planning. Mr. Baker was an incarnation of a real neighbor of mine when I was growing up. His family had a couple of dogs we would play with, and Mr. Baker and his wife were always very kind to us kids. Also, this gave me the chance to re-introduce Irene as Arnold's love interest. Named after "The woman," Irene Adler from A Scandal in Bohemia, she would be the perfect addition to what was starting to develop as a subplot.

Mid-summer Armadillo's Dream

The fourth connection was to William Shakespeare. It was here where my collaborations with my son began in more earnest. The challenge was to take a complicated story and reshape it into something kids would understand and enjoy. My kids wanted me to do Romeo and Juliet (the only play by Shakespeare of which they knew) but I reminded them that the play was a tragedy and didn't end well for Romeo or Juliet. I preferred the comedy, A Mid-summer Night's Dream. In the end, we combined the best of both into our story. The chapter is loaded with symbols. The "rose" in Arnold's rose colored glasses which were themselves adapted from Puck's little trick in A Mid-summer Night's Dream. The Robin is the symbol for such fairies who were used to cause the characters to act in certain ways beyond their senses – the rest of the story seemed to work well from there. I used various quotes from Romeo and Juliet, but choose to close the chapter with my favorite Shakespearian passage which is from the Tempest – illustrating how relative and temporary are our lives and also our problems. I hope it helps readers to put their troubles in perspective.

The Tell-Tale Armadillo

The fifth connection proved to be quite interesting. Edgar Allen Poe is not known for his happy stories and adapting the Tell-Tale Heart for a children's book produced an enjoyable challenge. So, the adaptation focuses on the theme of conscious. While there is a timeline throughout the book, which begins in spring and goes through summer (Mid-summer Night's Dream), and on through fall with this adaptation of The Tell-Tale Heart, each chapter can also more or less stand on its own as a short story. The Tell-Tale Armadillo reminds us that we all make mistakes and errors in judgment, just like Arnold. But in the end, it's what you make of those mistakes which is the truest testament of character.

Arnold in Slumberland

The sixth connection is to Winsor McCay's Little Nemo in Slumberland comic strip series. Upon reading the first draft of this chapter my son informed me that that it was, "The most entertaining." I became a fan of McCay's comic strips a few years ago after reading an article on him being the man who brought surrealism to popular culture via newspapers. His Nemo cartoons appeared in the early 1900's and were breakthroughs in many ways. The colors were revolutionary and the use of multiple panels was so new that they were actual numbered in his early cartoons. Every character and situation Arnold experiences in this chapter was inspired directly from McCay's cartoons. If you were to explore his work, you would certainly discover them. The one exception was that of the Squonk. The Squonk was my way of tipping my hat to my favorite rock band, Genesis. In 1976, they wrote a song titled, Squonk, which told of this creature who is so ugly that he weeps constantly which makes it easy for hunters to find him. Arnold's conversation with the Squonk was my son's favorite part. Also, it is thanks to Genesis that I heard of Winsor McCay in the first place. In 1978 they recorded a song called, Scenes from a Night's Dream, which featured many of McCay's cartoon concepts as well.

The Adventure of a Huckleberry Armadillo

The seventh connection was to Mark Twain's Huckleberry Finn. It wasn't hard to introduce a poor child named Huck and his dog Rags, who were running away. The local creek would stand in for the mighty Mississippi

River and its name was inspired by the creek which flowed through my neighborhood growing up. We would often play games in a neighbor's backyard along the creek, although we never had a boat. The knick names given to the two bullies (the King and the Duke) come directly from the swindlers Huck meets in the novel. The second adventure of being captured and plotting an escape was a bit more loosely based on Huck's escape during the novel's climax. Instead of Tom Sawyer returning to help him, I sent Otto in to assist. Boomer also shows up as the unlikely savior, but not before Arnold had already decided to sacrifice himself for his friends. Truly, at this point, the character of Arnold has really grown and I found myself excited that as the book progressed it was becoming more character driven – which meant to me that I was on to something greater than just adaptations of others' famous work.

Arnoldwulf

The eighth connection was clearly the story of Beowulf. I was tempted to try to write the entire chapter as an alliterative poem. But realizing that such a task would not only be daunting for me but also for the reader, I decided instead to introduce a new character who would speak in alliteration. Tiny Todd, was called on to recruit Arnold into coming to his neighborhood's rescue. Inspiration for the antagonist of this chapter came from my daughter who had drawn a beautiful illustration of a fox. From this drawing, I decided that Grumpy would be a fox. From there it was easy to connect with Beowulf by making the story about of a more rural neighborhood where chickens were being harassed by this fox, Grumpy. The sub-plot love story between Arnold and Irene also resurfaces.

The Face that Launched a Thousand Armadillos

The final connection was the piece de resistance. The Illiad was one of the earliest known epics, and so my son and I worked on how we might be able to adapt it in order to end the book with a scene of complete chaos. It had to be grand enough to reach some closure for Arnold, and it was clear that we'd have to use Mrs. Widmer to finish things off. This was Arnold's moment. He'd be the hero coming to Irene's rescue and dealing with his antagonist once and for all. But there was still the problem of how the book should end. We tossed around a few ideas, but in the end, we decided it would be best if Arnold and Irene decided to go back home and live like armadillos again. The rejection of the exciting world they had discovered existing all around them would hopefully also deliver a message that we all have our own special place in this world, and that your personal calling and heart is your truest guide.

Acknowledgements

Working on this book took many late nights, early mornings, and a lot of help and support from my kids, family, friends and colleagues. I particularly want to thank my awesome children for their participation and help in making this book possible. I also want to thank my parents for a lifetime of unconditional love and support. And thanks to my editors for all their diligence and skill in making my work look good.

Finally, a tribute to Arnold the Armadillo. It is funny how you can literally create a character out of thin air and breathe enough life into him to be able to evoke emotions in others – especially those of loyalty and love. Perhaps it is this very divine-like, creative quality which allows us to connect the themes of our lives to the greater purpose of life itself. Such is the gift of great literature. And while Arnold is merely a manifestation – a figment of my imagination, he has been set forth into the world to entertain and relate to children, letting them know that through life's struggles and hardships that they are not alone. You have friends all around you, even where you never imagined. I am forever grateful to him and all he has done for me and in helping to show my kids how much I love them.

Please SHARE this book with friends and family and write a review on Amazon.com!

Visit Arnold the Armadillo Online at:
www.facebook.com/ilovearnoldthearmadillo

♫ The Ballad of Arnold the Armadillo ♪

Words & Music by Paul Jannereth
Listen at, https://www.youtube.com/watch?v=I6Rm_kPLyrY
or scan the QR Code below.

His name is Arnold Armadillo
He's the very best friend you could have
When you need to talk or need a laugh
He'll say, "Sha-la-la-la-la-la"

He came through the garden bed
And with glasses on his head
All were shocked when they heard him talk
He said, "Sha-la-la-la-la-la"

♫ ♪ ♫ ♪

Now Arnold didn't always understand
All the ways of this strange new land
He'd learn a lot from trial and error
Shouting, "Sha-la-la-la-la-la"

He thought the windmill a monster

And the hound to be a great ghost
But from mistakes he learned the most
Singing, "Sha-la-la-la-la-la"

♫ ♪ ♫ ♪

Now Arnold never thought he'd fall in love
Until Robin helped him from above
But soon he knew what it was to have a broken heart
Crying, "Sha-la-la-la-la-la"

But in his wildest dreams
The world was not as it seemed
He saved the princess and found his heart
Loving, "Sha-la-la-la-la-la"

♫ ♪ ♫ ♪

So then Arnold knew what he had to do
To be a hero right and true
He went to help some other friends
Vowing, "Sha-la-la-la-la-la"

He saved little Rags from frightful Rex
And scared a fox to protect the rest
But you won't believe what happened next
He went, "Sha-la-la-la-la-la"

♫ ♪ ♫ ♪

His name is Arnold Armadillo
And he has a heart that's made of gold
When you need a laugh, or you need a smile
No matter if you're young or old

Just curl up with his book
And allow your mind to look
At how beautiful Arnold knows you are
And sing, "Sha-la-la-la-la-la"

♫ ♪ ♫ ♪

About the author

Paul Jannereth is originally from Grand Rapids, MI and obtained a degree in Education and History from Western Michigan University. He has also earned a Master's Degree in Educational Leadership from Michigan State University. He has made a career of teaching, financial services, and leadership development training.

For more information please visit
www.Facebook.com/bytheseapublications

by the sea ™

Publications

87873139R10128

Made in the USA
Columbia, SC
29 January 2018